Verity *felt a shaking in the tree under* her.

The duke was climbing nimbly toward her, the sun glinting off his golden hair.

"Good day to you, Miss Bascombe. Pass that creature down to me and I will take it to safety and return for you."

Verity lifted the cat and handed it to the duke. He swung nimbly to the ground and put the cat on the grass.

Verity leapt down into his arms and he held her very tightly against him. "You are safe now," he said softly. "There is nothing to fear."

But Verity had everything to fear. The violent wanton yearning of her body startled and alarmed her.

PRETTY POLLY

Marion Chesney

FAWCETT CREST • NEW YORK

A Fawcett Crest Book
Published by Ballantine Books
Copyright © 1988 by Marion Chesney

Library of Congress Catalog Card Number: 88-91117

ISBN 0-449-21343-9

Manufactured in the United States of America

First Edition: October 1988

PRETTY POLLY

PRETTY
POLLY

Chapter One

Mrs. Charlotte Manners was a pretty widow,
silly, vain, and ambitious. And yet she was clever
enough to admit to some limitations, two of them
being that her grammar was faulty and her spell-
ing slightly worse.

She was in sore need of an elegant letter writer.
The recipient of these letters was to be the Duke of
Denbigh.

When Charlotte was seventeen and the present
duke twenty-four, he had proposed to her and she
had refused him. For at that time, the duke had
been Lord Charles Stuart, the youngest son of a
notoriously clutch-fisted father. A Mr. Manners had
also proposed. At that time, the young Charlotte
had considered wealth to be a more desirable com-
modity than a title. Mr. Manners had been common
but vastly rich. He had paid no attention to the
unwritten social law that a man did not give a
young miss expensive presents and had showered
the dazzled Charlotte with expensive trinkets. And
so she had rejected Lord Charles and married Mr.
Manners. Mr. Manners had not lived very long af-

1

ter his marriage and Charlotte had been left a very wealthy widow.

She had just learned that a cholera epidemic had carried off Lord Charles's father and two elder brothers and that Lord Charles had become the Duke of Denbigh. Not only was he now one of the richest men in England but a duke as well.

Charlotte's spies told her that the duke was at his estates in the country. She planned to lure him back into London and into her arms. But to do that, she would need to write to him delicate letters, sweet letters that would reanimate his affections.

She sat in front of her mirror looking for inspiration in her own reflection. Charlotte often found her own beauty a great source of inspiration. If only I had studied harder at that stuffy seminary, she thought. Then her large blue eyes widened. What was the name of that vastly popular girl who had taken all the prizes? She got to her feet, went up to the attic, and opened the lid of one of the trunks stored there. Charlotte never threw anything away. She rummaged through piles of schoolbooks, children's books, novels, and sheet music until she found a notebook. It contained the names and addresses of her former classmates.

Her eye ran down the names, finally stopping at one. Verity Bascombe. That was it! Why not invite the poor thing to town for a visit? Verity had a modest background. She was a lawyer's daughter. She had never had much in the way of looks, and her dowry would be very small. Not married, most likely.

Charlotte carefully replaced all of the items in the trunk, except for the notebook, and then ran back down the stairs to write a letter. In writing to such a one as Verity Bascombe, there was no need to strive for elegance.

* * *

Verity Bascombe lived in a slim stone house on the outskirts of Market Basset, a small town near Bath. Her mother had died some years before, and Verity had remained with her father despite several proposals of marriage. Her quiet life suited her. She acted as hostess at her father's infrequent supper parties, attended church, was a member of the local sewing circle that made clothes for the poor, and read a great number of books from the circulating library. Recently, her father's behavior had made her begin to feel uneasy. Instead of being grateful to Verity for running his household competently, Mr. Bascombe had begun to point out that it was time she thought of setting up her own household. The first time he had voiced this, Verity had smiled, thinking that he would soon drop the subject. But he had returned to it the next day and the days after that. A promising young lawyer, George Carruthers, had taken to walking home with them after church on Sunday. Mr. Bascombe had said that Verity was not giving such a promising beau enough encouragement. She was twenty-four, her father had pointed out, and would soon be wearing caps.

Verity was not precisely beautiful. She had thick brown hair and black eyes that sparkled with intelligence. Her figure was neat, but a trifle short. She was somewhat thinner than was considered fashionably correct, and had no dimples on her elbows, a sad defect.

Everyone liked Verity. She was considered a cheerful, sensible lady. But no one knew of the passionate romantic that lurked inside Verity, the romantic who had turned down those proposals of marriage. Perhaps George Carruthers was her last

3

hope. He was all that was suitable. He belonged to the professional middle class, his legs were passable, and his skin, if a trifle sallow, was at least unmarked. He had a great deal of good sense, and no one knew that Verity was heartily tired of good sense, sound values, and a lack of humor.

But she privately thought that if she could depress Mr. Carruthers's hopes, then her father would become resigned to the idea of a spinster daughter. The only reason for marriage that Verity could see was to gain a comfortable home and independence, and she had both of those in her father's household.

The arrival of Charlotte's letter only caused a small ruffle in the tranquil pool of her life. Verity thought of the spoiled seminary brat that had been Charlotte, put the letter aside so that she could send a refusal later in the day, and continued to eat her breakfast.

Mr. Bascombe looked at the discarded letter with a certain amount of irritation. It was a very unusual event for a letter from London to arrive in Market Basset and he thought Verity might at least have volunteered to tell him who it was from.

"Verity," he said sharply. "I remark you have received a letter from London!"

"Yes, Papa."

"From whom?"

"No one of importance," Verity said placidly. "A girl who was at the seminary in Bath the same time as I has written to ask me to visit her in London."

"Where in London?"

"Berkeley Square."

"Berkeley Square! That is the best address in England! Who is she?"

"She is now a Mrs. Charlotte Manners and is a widow, and, I believe, extremely rich. I am always reading about her in the social columns. When I knew her, she was the Honorable Charlotte Parren."

"An aristocrat?"

"Yes, Papa, and a very pampered and spoiled one."

Mr. Bascombe took a deep breath. "You will go, of course."

"No," said Verity, surprised. "I was not a particular friend of Charlotte's. Besides, the idea of staying for any length of time with some stranger is fatiguing."

"I have made up my mind: You are to go," said Mr. Bascombe. "I have long wished to travel to Edinburgh to stay with an old friend. This is my opportunity. I shall go when you go to London."

"But—"

"I said, you will go!" shouted Mr. Bascombe. "I had ambitions for you when I sent you to that expensive seminary in Bath. I thought you would make useful friends. But I've watched you turn down invitation after invitation. I am not going to go to my grave feeling that if it had not been for me you would have been married with children."

"I did not accept any of those invitations because the girls who sent them to me were far above me in social rank. I would have felt sadly at a loss in any of their great mansions. We manage very comfortably, Papa. There is no reason for me to marry."

Mr. Bascombe played his ace. "Oh, yes, there is," he said. "I want to get married myself."

"You never told me. Who is this lady?"

Mr. Bascombe thought wildly of all the marriageable ladies of their acquaintance. "Miss Emily Butterworth," he said at last.

"Emily is a year younger than I!"

5

"I like 'em young," her father said brutally.

Verity felt her ordered world caving in under her feet. Of course any new wife of Papa's would not want an unmarried daughter in residence! And a new mistress of the household would expect to handle the reins herself.

She studied her father for some moments and then said, "You are very anxious I should accept this invitation. Why?"

"Because if the men don't suit you here, mayhap they'll suit you there," howled Mr. Bascombe.

"But I shall be meeting members of the aristocracy and they only marry beneath them if the girl has a great deal of money, which I do not have. And I am not beautiful."

Mr. Bascombe clutched what was left of his hair and gave it a hard tug. Although she was his daughter, he knew what it was about Verity that had drawn so many proposals of marriage. There was a sensuality about her, a strong, almost animal attraction that had long worried him. He suspected his daughter of harboring strong passions beneath her outwardly chaste bosom, the sort of passions that might cause her one day to lose her virginity to someone totally unsuitable.

Two years ago, he had taken Verity on a little drive to view a ruined church a few miles outside the town. On the way there, they had stopped for refreshment at a fashionable posting house. The prices had been dreadfully steep and the staff insolent. In the coffee room had been a party of men. One of them had been extremely handsome and rakish. Mr. Bascombe remembered him well. He had been about six feet tall and exquisitely dressed. He had powerful shoulders, excellent legs, and a clear skin. His eyes were hard and predatory, and his nose thin, high-bridged, and arrogant. His mouth was well-shaped, and his chin, strong and firm. His hair was golden, thick, and curly. In all, he was one of the best-looking and most decadent Adonises that Mr. Bascombe had ever seen.

Mr. Bascombe had been too flustered in dealing with the uppity waiters to quite take in what was happening, but when Verity's jug of lemonade had finally been placed in front of her, he noticed that she had a delicate color and that her black eyes were sparkling.

The Adonis was not listening to his friends. He was leaning back in his chair, surveying Verity with a hard, assessing, hawklike look, and Verity was very much aware of his gaze. Mr. Bascombe's sensible daughter appeared all at once flustered and very feminine.

The waiter had failed to bring their cold collation. Mr. Bascombe returned to the battle, only to find the Adonis had risen to his feet. In a chilly voice, he had told the staff to jump to it, to serve Mr. Bascombe at the double. The difference was amazing. Mr. Bascombe and Verity were immediately surrounded by scraping and bowing servants. When Mr. Bascombe finally tried to pay, he was told their refreshments were "on the house," with the compliments of the owner.

Mr. Bascombe had looked suspiciously at the tall Adonis, who had smiled back lazily. Mr. Bascombe was sure he had paid their shot.

Verity had been dreamy and distracted for days afterward while her father had reflected sourly that he was glad that at least one man, however unsuitable, had sparked some interest in his normally infuriatingly sensible daughter.

He did not expect Verity to find a beau in London. But he did think that closer contact with the type of aristocrat who seemed to rouse her might then mean she would come home prepared to marry someone of her own class. Mr. Bascombe thought he would be failing in his duty if Verity were allowed to remain unwed. Besides, that seminary in Bath had cost a fortune, and he would like to boast to his friends about his daughter's aristocratic friends—the reason he had sent her there in the first place. Mr. Bascombe worshipped the aristocracy and thought that anyone coming into contact with such gods would catch godlike qualities himself, as if by a sort of osmosis.

Verity so far forgot herself as to put her elbows on the table. She leaned toward her father. "Had you not better start to go out walking with Miss Emily, Papa, or something like that. I have hardly ever seen you even speak to her."

"Emily and I have seen quite a lot of each other," lied her father. "I shall pop the question as soon as I return from Edinburgh. Now, I know you will behave like a good daughter and not let any selfish wish stand in the way of my plans."

Verity was torn between exasperation and amusement. She was now sure that her father did not want to marry again. She was also sure that he did not even want to go to Edinburgh. On the other hand, it might do him good to try to run the household without her.

She decided to go to London and endure a few weeks of Charlotte's company. When she returned, she was sure her father would be so grateful to see her he would drop all this marriage nonsense—that is, if by any chance he might happen to be serious—and would no longer talk of either marriage for her or marriage for himself.

Marry Emily Butterworth! Fustian. Papa was all

of forty-five years old. How could he expect her to believe such a farrago of lies.

Some imp of mischief prompted Verity to approach Emily later that day in the circulating library. She told Emily of her proposed visit to London. Emily was a merry, bouncing sort of girl who wore a great number of ribbons. She had ribbons in her hat and shoulder knots on her dress and little bunches of ribbons at her hem. She had wide china blue eyes that surveyed the world with innocent good humor. Her parents were in very straitened circumstances, which was why Emily was still unwed.

Emily exclaimed with delight and made Verity promise to keep a diary so that she might read all the descriptions of grand *ton* parties to the sewing circle on her return.

"I do not want to go," said Verity, "but poor Papa is telling me stories to force me to go. He even said he was going to marry you!"

Emily's round face turned pink. "How very flattering," she gasped. "Did he mean it?"

Verity was about to laugh with scorn and say no. But something held her back. Emily's eyes were shining and her plump fingers, holding a library book, were tightly clenched.

"I think you will need to find out for yourself," said Verity slowly. "I must go, Emily. I have many chores."

Verity looked carefully at her father at supper that evening. He was a small man with a slim, wiry figure and the same black eyes as his daughter. He was quite handsome although his hair was thin, thought Verity. But, goodness, he was so very much older than Emily. The whole idea was ridiculous and Verity wished she had never teased Emily on the subject.

9

Three weeks later, Verity Bascombe traveled to London on the mail coach and then took a hack from the City of London to the West End.

Charlotte's house looked very imposing. Verity glanced down at her pelisse and gown, which had looked so modish when she had left Market Basset and suddenly felt shabby.

To her relief, although Charlotte was out walking, she was received by the servants with every flattering courtesy. Her bedchamber was prettily decorated with flowered wallpaper, and had one of the latest design of beds, without posts or canopy. By the window was a very large desk with an enormous inkwell and sheets and sheets of blank parchment. It was odd to see such a desk in a bedchamber.

The butler had told her that tea would be served in the drawing room in half an hour, the time Charlotte was expected to return.

Verity brushed her hair, washed her face and hands, changed her gown for one of blue muslin, rang the bell for a footman, and was conducted to the drawing room.

The smell of the drawing room and its occupants made her take a nervous step back.

"Mrs. Manners's pets," said the footman. "Not savage, miss. Quite docile."

Wondering, Verity went into the room. "That one's dead," said the footman, moving past her to where a pathetic little corpse lay on the hearthrug. "I'll just take the nasty thing away." The "nasty thing" was a dead monkey dressed in a red jacket.

A French greyhound limped forward on its spindly legs. It was as fat as a barrel and its coat was dull. On a perch by the fireplace stood an enormous mangy parrot staring at Verity out of strange, clever, reptilian eyes. On the sofa lay a large cat, its eyes half closed. It looked near death. Verity stroked it and said, "Poor pussy," and the cat roused itself and bit her hand.

Rubbing her hand and hoping the animal wasn't rabid, Verity turned her attention to the parrot. She scratched its head feathers. It hopped down on her shoulder, dug its talons in, and leaned against her hair, giving a strange crooning noise at the back of its throat.

Verity tried to dislodge it, for it was very heavy and smelly, but it only gripped harder. Its feathers were scarlet and gray, but it had a strange golden fringe on its legs. It was like no parrot that Verity had ever seen.

Charlotte's voice sounded from the hall. The parrot, hopping back up on its perch, stood motionless.

A vision of golden curls, rose-leaf complexion, and wide blue eyes tripped into the room. "Verity, my love," cried Charlotte Manners. "How wonderful to see you. Are you content with your room?"

She hugged Verity, who had risen to meet her, and Verity, surprised and pleased with the warmth of the reception, smiled at Charlotte.

"You have not changed a bit," cried Charlotte. "Have I?"

"Yes," said Verity truthfully. "You are more beautiful than ever."

"Oh, we are going to have such *fun*," cried Charlotte. She sat down carelessly on top of the cat and then leaped up again in a fury. The cat had bitten her.

Charlotte rang the bell. When the butler answered it, she said, "Get rid of this zoo, Pomfret. Nasty, smelly things. They bore me."

"Where shall I put them, ma'am?"

"In the dust bin."

"Very good, ma'am," said the butler, advancing cautiously on the parrot, which leaped onto Verity's shoulder, making her stagger under its weight.

Verity thought of the poor monkey. She was very sentimental about birds and animals, a weakness of which she was thoroughly ashamed. Considering animals as pets was a decadent luxury when there were so many children starving to death.

But somehow Verity found herself saying, "I wonder, Charlotte . . . I may call you that?"

"By all means, dear Verity," cooed Charlotte. Verity's remark about her being more beautiful had pleased her greatly.

"If you would let me take care of the dog and cat and bird," said Verity, "I think I could restore them to health."

"As you wish," said Charlotte with a wave of her hand. "That parrot cost a fortune and it never says a word. Tiresome, ugly thing."

The butler looked relieved.

"I wish you would go back to your perch," said Verity to the parrot. "What is its name, Charlotte?"

"The villain who sold it to me said it was called Pretty Polly. Stoopid name for an evil-looking bird."

"Go back to your perch, Pretty Polly," said Verity, trying to shrug the parrot off.

To her amazement, the parrot promptly flew to its perch, cocked its head on one side, and regarded her with an almost paternal eye.

"It seems to like you," said Charlotte. "But if you want to look after the things, Verity, they have to go in your room."

"Very well," said Verity, looking at the small

zoo with a sinking heart. "I know the correct feeding for cats and dogs, but what do you feed a parrot?"

"*I* don't know," said Charlotte crossly. "I must have fed that bird a ton of sugar plums and yet never a word did it say."

Which, thought Verity, probably explains the mangy condition of the bird.

"I am afraid your little monkey is dead."

"Where is it?" asked Charlotte, peering under the chairs and sofa.

"The footman took it away."

"Good. You can't trust servants these days. They might have left it somewhere to rot and it would smell so. I must leave you soon, dear Verity, but we shall have a long coze on the morrow. Lord Strangeworth is coming to take me to a *fête champêtre* in the Surrey fields."

"You hinted in your letter," said Verity, "that I might be of use to you in some way."

"First of all I want you to solve a mystery for me," said Charlotte. "I am very beautiful and very rich."

Verity blinked at this piece of vanity and decided Charlotte had not changed from the spoiled brat of the seminary. "Two gentlemen have come to propose to me this year. On each occasion, when I descended to the drawing room to accept their offer, they ran past me, babbling about another appointment, and neither has come near me since. I want you to find out why. One is called Sir Brian Vincent and the other Lord Chalton. But do not spend too much time over that. I am after bigger game."

"Indeed?"

"The present Duke of Denbigh proposed to me when he was a mere younger son without much money. I refused him. Now, of course, the situation is altered. I am a widow, beautiful, attractive, and prepared to reanimate his affections. The irritating man shows no signs of coming to London for the Season. That is your job!"

"But what can I do?"

"Dear Verity, you must write letters for me, winning, amusing, charming letters to draw him back."

"Very well," said Verity, relieved that the task was so easy. "When would you like me to begin?"

"As soon as you have rested," said Charlotte after a little pause, during which she had been about to command Verity to begin right away. But she was very pleased with Verity. Charlotte was not popular with her own sex, and for the moment, the novelty of having a female companion of her own age pleased her.

"I shall go and change," said Charlotte. "Do not forget to take these creatures to your room, Verity, else I shall have them destroyed."

She dropped a light kiss on Verity's cheek and tripped from the room.

Verity looked at the cat, the dog, and the parrot. She gave a little sigh and rang the bell. When Pomfret, the butler, answered it, Verity shyly asked him for two leashes, one for the dog and one for the cat. "And, Pomfret," she said "I would be most grateful if you could find out for me what is suitable food for a parrot and purchase it for me. The cat is to be fed a small amount of plain, boiled fish and given a spoonful of fish oil. No milk. Just plain water. The dog, I think, plain oatmeal with some vegetables and gravy and a bowl of water. I shall be keeping them in my room. Am I asking too much of you? In a household this size you must have many chores to occupy your time."

"I shall be glad to oblige, miss," said Pomfret with a wooden face.

I should not have apologized. How he must despise me, thought Verity—not knowing Pomfret was shortly to tell the staff that it was a great relief to serve a *lady* for a change.

When the leashes were produced, Verity stood and then winced as the parrot hopped onto her shoulder. "I will need to find a piece of leather for my shoulder, Pomfret," said Verity ruefully, "until I can train this bird. What are the names of the dog and the cat?"

"The cat is called Fluff and the dog Frou Frou."

"I think I shall change their names, you know," said Verity. "Something more ordinary, I think."

"Mrs. Manners changed the names," said Pomfret. "The cat was called Peter and the dog Tray."

"Well, Peter and Tray they shall be once more. I think fresh air would do them all good. Hyde Park is near here, is it not?"

"Yes, miss. Go right along to the end of Mount Street and across Park Lane."

The parrot gave Verity's hair a peck and flew back to its perch.

"I would leave the bird's perch in here at the moment, Pomfret," said Verity uneasily.

"Seems to have taken a great fancy to you, miss, if I may say so."

Verity looked at Pretty Polly doubtfully.

"If you are going out walking, miss, I will tell James, the second footman, to attend you."

"I trust the young man will not find the expedition too humiliating," said Verity. "Very well, tell James I shall be ready to set out in ten minutes."

When Verity had put on a warm, if unfashionable, wool cloak, she returned to the drawing room.

The house was large and she had no idea where Charlotte's apartments were.

She put a leash on the cat.

James, the second footman, was a magnificent creature in scarlet livery. "I have never seen a cat on a leash before, miss," he volunteered.

"Neither have I," said Verity cheerfully. "But we must try." She put the other leash on Tray, and dragging the cat and leading the dog, she made for the street door. The great parrot sailed off its perch and landed on her shoulder with a thump.

"Oh, no," said Verity. "Not you. But I suppose my thick cloak will protect me from your talons."

The first footman rushed to open the door and Verity handed the dog's leash to James. "If you will gently walk the dog, James, I will try to cope with the cat."

The butler stood on the step, watching with amusement as the odd procession made its way slowly down Mount Street.

The day was brisk and sunny with great flying clouds. Verity thought Londoners were a very *staring* sort of people. Quizzing glasses were raised. People stopped in their tracks. They didn't say anything. They just stared.

Pretty Polly did an ecstatic little shuffling dance on Verity's shoulder, and she groaned. The cat sat down for the umpteenth time, so she stooped, nearly falling over under the weight of the great parrot, and scooped it up in her arms, hoping it would not bite.

The vast, treeless expanse of the middle of Hyde Park came as a delight to Verity. She walked past the round reservoir, leading her odd menagerie until she found a seat by a footpath. She sat down, slipped the cat's leash, and set it down. She then unfastened the dog's leash. The dog immediately

16

ran around in circles, barking with delight, and then fell panting at Verity's feet, its sides heaving. The cat slouched off and disappeared from view. The parrot sailed off into the air.

"Now what am I to do, James?" asked Verity.

"I wouldn't worry, miss," said James, standing at attention behind Verity's seat. "If they don't come back, Mrs. Manners will not be upset. Awful mess they make. Not house-trained, if you take my meaning."

"Oh, dear, the cat must be allowed out at all times and the dog must have regular walks."

"Mr. Pomfret has sent for a veterinary surgeon, miss, to help you with the parrot's feed."

"How very good of him, James. I confess country people such as I do not expect such thoughtfulness from Londoners."

"I am from the country myself," said James.

"Indeed! Will you not sit down, James? The day is quite hot and it must be extremely tiring to stand there."

"Thank you, miss, but it's not done."

"Oh, I am not the complete country bumpkin," Verity said easily. "I know *that*, but there is no one around."

James's feet hurt. He had been running errands all morning. He cautiously edged around the seat and sat down gingerly next to Verity.

Soon, he was responding to Verity's questions about his country home. James had been drawn to London by the thought of working in a London mansion and of the livery he would wear. But it had, so far, been a difficult and strange existence. He thought that his quiet conversation with Verity in the middle of Hyde Park in the sunshine was one of the most pleasant things that had happened to him since he had come to town.

Verity took respect from servants as a matter of course. She treated her own small staff with friendly courtesy and kindness and never realized it was her own manner and behavior that brought out the best in them. She had, however, expected London servants to be very stuffy and grand and was pleasantly surprised by Charlotte's staff.

As the shadows began to lengthen across the grass, Verity awoke the now sleeping Tray. "Perhaps I will return this evening and see if I can find the other two," she said uneasily.

James took the leash from her and they both walked slowly toward the lodge at Park Lane, for the poor dog was so fat it could hardly move. There was a sudden whirr of wings and then Pretty Polly landed with a thump on Verity's shoulder. "Well, that's one, anyway, James," she said cheerfully.

James looked back. "I'm blessed," he said. "Here comes t'other."

Peter, the cat, came skulking up behind them. Verity bent down to put on its leash, but it bared its teeth, hissed a warning, and backed away.

Verity walked on, looking back from time to time, and found to her surprise that the cat was following at a distance. When they got to the end of Mount Street, she looked back. Peter was lying stretched out in the middle of the pavement. She ran back, picked the cat up, and patted its dusty black fur.

A low, creaky, whirring sound, like the sound made by a rusty clockwork toy, came from somewhere inside the cat's body. The dreadful Peter was purring.

Feeling a warm sense of achievement, Verity

conducted her small menagerie back inside the house.

Now to send off that first letter.

Chapter Two

Verity sat at the huge oak pedestal desk in her room, chewing the end of a quill pen. Lying stretched out on the far side of the desk was the cat. The dog lay curled at her feet. Both animals had been examined by a veterinary surgeon. He had agreed with Verity's ideas on diet, dosed both animals with sulfur powder, and then recommended a purge. But Verity could not face the idea of a night in her bedchamber with two purged and unhouse-trained animals and so had refused. Sunflower seeds and fresh fruit had been provided for the parrot.

Pretty Polly had fascinated the vet. He had kept shaking his head and saying he had never seen a bird quite like it. It was very large, even for a parrot, and he had been intrigued by the gold fringe of fine feathers on the bird's legs, which gave it the peculiar appearance of being dressed in exotic and ragged knee breeches.

Verity had then had supper served on a tray and found herself free at last to begin her task.

In order to do her best for Charlotte and repay her hospitality, there must be something in the letters that would make the duke want to return to London. He had once proposed to Charlotte. He might still be in love with her. Verity frowned. But surely aristocrats did not fall in love. Marriages were more like business partnerships than marriages of true minds. On the other hand, the duke had only been twenty-four when he had proposed and Charlotte seventeen, so perhaps it *had* been love.

At last she decided that the first letter should simply be one of condolence. He had recently lost both brothers and father.

She wrote a short letter, remembering her own grief at the death of her mother and putting a great deal of warmth and sympathy into her sentences.

She had just finished it when Charlotte came into the room. "Oh, you have begun work already, you dearest of creatures," cried Charlotte. She looked a picture in white spotted muslin with a very high waist and a very low neckline. However, Verity privately thought that Charlotte's enormous bonnet, lined with pink-and-black-striped taffeta and tied under her chin with broad ribbons of the same material, was a trifle garish.

Charlotte picked up the letter and read it and made a moue of disappointment. "Not very loverlike, Verity," she commented.

"I could not really write anything else," said Verity. "When he replies, I shall send a further letter and try to charm him for you. But, in the circumstances, I could hardly write anything of a light and flirtatious nature. It would look most odd."

Charlotte, who had been scowling horribly, suddenly smiled. "You always were a clever puss. I shall trust your judgment. Now, Lord Chalfont is to call tomorrow and I know he means to propose."

21

"Then there is no need to write to the duke," exclaimed Verity.

"Pooh! I am not going to *accept* Chalfont. It will do my standing in society no harm to be followed around by a languishing and rejected beau. Faith, but it was tedious today. I wish you had been with me. But why not! I mean, why not accompany me on some of my jaunts. Kean is playing Richard III tomorrow, and I have a box."

"I should like that above all things," said Verity, her eyes shining. "Oh, to see a Shakespeare play on the stage."

"Silly widgeon. Who looks or listens to the play? Society goes to see each other. But you shall come and I shall point out all the quizzes to you. I see you have got rid of that pesky parrot."

"I wouldn't dream of doing such a thing without your permission, Charlotte. It is on its perch in the drawing room. I did not want to move it until it became accustomed to me. I wonder, Charlotte, while we are on the subject of Pretty Polly, whether we might have a cage for the bird?"

"Why? Has it become violent?"

Verity suppressed a grin. She had a sudden mental picture of a parrot wielding an ax. "No, but a cage is more easily cleaned of bird droppings than the drawing-room floor."

"As you will. Chalfont is to call at noon. We shall go down together and you shall see how prettily I break his heart."

Charlotte kissed Verity and sailed out and then let out a slight scream as Pretty Polly sailed in. The parrot flew straight to the rail at the top of Verity's bed and shuffled up and down. She turned in the doorway. "If I were you, Verity, I would poison that ugly bird."

Verity bit back an angry reply. She had no patience with people who made pets of birds and animals only to lose interest in them.

"In any case, I must get a good night's sleep and be prepared to break Chalfont's heart."

"Is he handsome?" asked Verity curiously.

"Chalfont, handsome?" Charlotte gave a tinkling laugh, that fashionable laugh that young ladies practiced as assiduously as their pianoforte lessons. It was supposed to start at the top register and cascade down the scale with a "chiming" sound. "My dear, he is the veriest quiz and *such* a bore. He wears false calves. Do not worry. My refusal of his suit will not dent his massive vanity one whit."

Charlotte went out and closed the door.

Verity decided to undress and go to bed. She was just twisting around to unfasten the tapes of her gown when she met the unblinking stare of three pairs of eyes. There was a screen folded in the corner of the room. She pulled it forward and went behind it to undress, feeling silly but reflecting that she would feel even sillier undressing before the interested gazes of Charlotte's pets.

She climbed into bed and stretched out luxuriously. The bed was very comfortable. There was a soft thump as the cat landed on the bed beside her and started doing a mad dance on the coverlet, digging its claws in and out, its eyes shut in ecstasy.

"Shoo!" said Verity, waving a hand at the cat, which seized and bit it. Verity picked up her book from the bedside table and thumped the cat on the head, and it slunk off the bed.

The grating sound of the watch calling the hour awoke Verity during the night. She groaned and turned over and found the cat lying on the pillow next to her. She was going to throw it off the bed, but there was something comforting and soothing

about its purring, so she closed her eyes and let it
stay where it was.

The next day, Lord Chalfont stood in Charlotte's
drawing room and studied his reflection in the looking glass. "Fine. You're looking very fine," he told
himself aloud. He felt his new wasp-waisted coat
did him justice, and his skintight pantaloons were
drawn over his false wooden calves, making him
feel like some muscular Greek god.

A huge parrot sailed into the room and landed on
its perch with a thump. It stared unblinkingly at
Lord Chalfont, who looked at it uneasily. "Bloody
parrot," he said.

"Pretty Polly," said the parrot in a harsh parrot
voice. Then it put its head on one side, and in an
uncanny imitation of Charlotte's voice, it said,
"Chalfont, handsome? My dear, he is the veriest
quiz and *such* a bore. Do not worry. My refusal of
his suit will not dent his massive vanity one whit."

Charlotte and Verity were descending the stairs
during Pretty Polly's speech. They looked at each
other in surprise as they heard the faint sound of a
female voice coming from the drawing room.

But before they could reach the door of the drawing room, it opened and Lord Chalfont came storm-
ing out.

He stopped short at the sight of them. "Good day,
madam," he shouted. "A *very* good day to you."

"Why are you leaving, my lord?" asked Charlotte, amazed.

"Because, madam, there is nothing for me here!"
Lord Chalfont stalked toward the street door just
as a footman sprang to open it. One of his false
calves slipped and he went off with it bulging above
his ankle.

Charlotte and Verity retreated to the drawing

room where they stared at each other in amazement. "You see, Verity?" said Charlotte. "It has
happened again. Who was that woman we heard
speaking?" She rang the bell and questioned the
butler closely. But Pomfret could only shake his
head in bewilderment. Only Lord Chalfont had gone
into the drawing room and only Lord Chalfont had
come out of it.

"Perhaps the place is haunted," said Charlotte
with a shiver.

Verity looked at Pretty Polly. "Perhaps the parrot can talk."

"Pooh! Not that stupid bird. And even if it could,
it would have a squawking parroty voice."

"Perhaps I should try to ask Lord Chalfont what
happened," volunteered Verity. "Will he be at the
play this evening?"

"He said he was going," said Charlotte, biting
her fingernails. "Fiddle. I hate mysteries. Would
you say there was something *repellent* about me,
Verity?"

"Not in the slightest," said Verity, for what else
could she say to her young hostess? But when she
was alone later she thought about the problem.
Charlotte was vain and self-centered, but very
beautiful. She appeared to view men in the light of
providers of titles and money. She did not pretend
to have any finer feelings, and surely that was to
her credit. Verity recalled the conversations of the
young misses at the seminary. Dowries, land, and
titles were discussed at great length. Of course they
all read romances and sighed over dream heroes,
but each girl obviously knew her duty to her parents, which was to secure an eligible man and in-
crease the prestige of the family. Love was
something one found outside of marriage.

Verity had not thought of the gentleman she had

seen in the posting house for some time. Now, his face was once more vividly in front of her. She could see that lazy smile, hear that mocking voice, and see the sun shining through the coffee-room window on that golden hair. It occurred to her that such a splendid creature would surely be in London for the Season. She might even see him again.

Pretty Polly looked at her cynically and strode up and down the desk, the parrot's wings making it look like a fussy old gentleman in a tail coat.

"You're probably right," said Verity. "Bound to be married by now. Probably was married then."

The Duke of Denbigh was in a very bad mood. He was tired of his staff and neighbors trying to block any innovations by telling him his father would "turn in his grave." The duke had a macabre picture of his father's corpse revolving furiously like a busy drill until he surfaced in Australia to startle the aborigines.

The duke had not been very close to his father or to his brothers, who had been some ten years older than he. And yet he felt their loss, combined with a strong feeling of guilt that he should have survived.

He shuffled through the morning's post, dividing it into neat piles of bills to be paid, social invitations, requests for money, and personal letters. He had pensioned off his late father's elderly secretary, who had been foremost in the father-revolving-in-the-grave school of thought.

Among the personal letters were many delicately scented ones, reminding him coyly of the time he had danced with Miss This or Miss That. He had nearly run out of patience by the time he reached the Verity-Charlotte missive.

His eye fell on the signature at the bottom and

he experienced a feeling of distaste. That he had ever proposed marriage to such an empty-headed creature as Charlotte was a source of shame. He glanced at the first sentence and his thin eyebrows rose. He was amazed that a woman like Charlotte would have the good taste to sympathize with him on his bereavement. He read on. The tenderness and the sympathy in the letter touched his heart. Perhaps he had not been such a young fool after all.

He pushed the other letters aside and began to write a short reply.

The visit to the play engendered in Verity the beginnings of liking and affection for Charlotte Manners. For a Charlotte who could so casually open the door to such miracles was a Charlotte to inspire gratitude.

Edmund Kean had just arrived on the London stage to dazzle and amaze audiences. He was no Romeo, no Hamlet; because he was small and had a harsh voice, he had to be Shylock, Richard III, Iago, or Macbeth.

For once, the London audience did not eye each other or chatter. For once, even the busy, noisy prostitutes were silent.

The poet, Samuel Taylor Coleridge, had declared that "to see Kean act is like reading Shakespeare by flashes of lightning." Kean's huge personality dominated the theater. He released a tremendous force. He *was* Richard: hunchbacked, evil, plotting, yet every inch a king.

At the interval, Charlotte's box was crowded with admirers, but Verity barely noticed them. She sat in a daze, waiting for the play to begin again.

When it was all over, she turned to Charlotte,

tears glittering in her eyes, and said simply, "Thank you."

"*Stoopid*," said Charlotte, but looking pleased. "*I*, for one, do not know what people see in the man. He is so little and insignificant and not at all pleasing to the eye. Lord Chalfont is not here. Fiddle. If only I knew what on earth had happened. Perhaps he is mad. Perhaps he talks to himself when he is alone in a falsetto voice like a woman's."

As they made their way out of the playhouse, Verity, released from the spell cast by Kean, was able to observe Charlotte's behavior when she stopped to exchange greetings with various gentlemen. She had to admit she could find little fault with it. Charlotte glowed with beauty; her eyes were amused and flirtatious. It was only when one gentleman introduced his sister that Verity observed Charlotte's eyes becoming bored and noticed how she barely gave the young miss a civil reply. Charlotte had little time for her own sex, unless they could be used.

But Verity, still elated by the performance, could not find any hideous character defects. Charlotte was spoiled by her great beauty to a certain extent, but she was surely no worse than many of the other ladies in the Season whose sole concern was to find a husband.

But their friendship was to receive a blow in a very short time.

Verity had a restless night and awoke just as dawn was breaking. The sun was streaming through the slats in the venetian blinds.

She decided to take her zoo for a promenade in the gardens in Berkeley Square. There was no need to take a footman. No one would be about.

She dressed and walked out into the fresh air,

followed by the dog and the cat and with the parrot nestling on her shoulder.

But Verity did not know that dawn was the time when the bucks and bloods of London were usually heading homeward. She had just entered the gardens and was walking under the young plane trees when a party of noisy and drunken bloods entered the square.

They saw Verity dressed in her old cloak and with her hair down her back, saw the parrot, the dog, and the cat, and thought she was some maid sent out with her mistress's pets.

There were three of them, their eyes red with drink, their faces gross and swollen. They were dressed like coachmen, with many capes to their coats and many strings to their knee breeches.

"Let's have some sport with the pretty maid," cried one.

"Keep your distance, sirs," said Verity haughtily.

This brought roars of laughter. One darted forward and tried to lift Verity's skirts with his sword stick. She slapped him and then found another had caught her around the waist.

"Help!" screamed Verity.

The parrot, which had flown off her shoulder at the beginning of the attack, suddenly dived like a hawk, talons outstretched. The man holding Verity cried with alarm and released his hold. Another was savagely bitten in the ankle by the cat. They started to run from the square. Pretty Polly dived again, seized the leader's hat and wig, and tore them off. The parrot tried the same ploy with one of the others, who unfortunately was wearing his own hair and who started to scream when the puzzled bird tried to rip it off. Emboldened by the men's terror, the dog, Tray, leaped, snapping, into the fray, and the hullabaloo rose to the heavens. Charlotte's servants came running out armed with sticks and finished the rout.

Panting and disheveled, Verity walked into the house to find a very angry Charlotte, in her nightgown and negligee, waiting in the hall.

"You should know better, Verity," said Charlotte, "than to go roistering with the men of the town. Have you no thought for *my* reputation? Fie! For shame."

"I was attacked, Charlotte. Brutally attacked."

"Fiddle!"

"Charlotte, how can you be so cruel and unkind?"

"My name, else you had forgot, is Mrs. Manners."

Verity gave her a look of contempt and went on up to her room with dog, cat, and parrot and locked herself in.

"Hoity-toity miss," said Charlotte petulantly. "Well, she can pack and leave this very day." Then she went back to bed and back to sleep with nothing on her conscience to trouble her.

She awoke at noon and rang for her chocolate, which was brought to her with the morning post. The first thing she saw was a letter with Denbigh's seal on it.

With an exclamation, she ripped it open.

"Dear Mrs. Manners," Denbigh had written:

Your warm and sympathetic letter pleased me greatly. In fact, you are the only person who has had the good taste to commiserate with me rather than to congratulate me.

I have much work to do here, my servants regarding change as being next to Jacobinism!

*I appreciate your views that the pleasures of
the Season, though trivial, can help to
alleviate grief. But I must confess, however, to
having taken the Season in dislike. What else
is there but vanity and malicious gossip?*

*You have made me feel guilty. You, too,
have felt the grief of loss, and yet I did not
honor you with the courtesy of a letter of
condolence. Please forgive me. Your words
have brought me great comfort.*

Yr. humble servant,

Denbigh

"Drat and double drat," said Charlotte aloud. "I
was rude to her, I think. But she will understand."
Anything waking Charlotte from a deep sleep put
her in a foul temper, but she assumed that everyone was like that and therefore everyone should
understand.

Verity was regretting having paid the vet herself. She was counting her small stock of pin money
and reflecting that the mail coach, besides being
very expensive, would not relish the presence of cat,
dog, and parrot inside. She would need to go by
stagecoach, and the menagerie would need to travel
with her on the roof. Verity did not really want to
be burdened with Charlotte's pets, but she was sure
they would be destroyed if she left them behind.

Two housemaids were packing her clothes; the
butler, Pomfret, was scratching the parrot's head;
James, the second footman, was crouched on the
floor, putting air holes in a box to make a carrying
case for the cat; the housekeeper, Mrs. Andrew, was
fussing about, trying to get Verity to eat; and the
first footman, Paul, was trying to get her attention
so that he could brag about the neat traveling box

of bird seed and animal food that he had made up for the journey.

"What is all this?" demanded Charlotte, looking at them all.

"We are helping Miss Bascombe to prepare for the journey," said the butler.

Charlotte ran forward and hugged Verity. "Oh, you silly puss. How missish of you to take me so seriously. I am cross as crabs when I am awakened. Go away, all of you, and leave us in peace."

When the servants had left, Verity said in a firm voice, "Your behavior is not acceptable, Mrs. Manners. I was attacked this morning, and had it not been for the brave behavior of your pets, I shudder to think what would have happened to me."

Charlotte looked at her in alarm. "Why do you call me Mrs. Manners?"

"You told me to this morning."

"Oh, this morning I was a beast. Listen, my friend, I am a monster when I am awakened. I deeply apologize for my behavior. Come, we shall go driving this afternoon and buy a cage for your parrot."

Verity gave a reluctant smile. "*Your* parrot, Charlotte."

"Oh, say you will accept my apology. Dear Verity, my heart is wrung."

Verity hesitated. She had had a letter from her father in which he said he would be setting out for Scotland in a week's time, after shutting up the house and giving the servants a leave of absence. After a week, she would not have another chance to leave until his return. And yet . . . Charlotte did seem so genuinely contrite.

"Then I shall stay," said Verity.

Verity enjoyed the drive, enjoyed Charlotte's

prattle and the fun they had choosing a magnificent cage for the large parrot.

She was comfortable she had made the right decision in promising to stay. I believe Charlotte is really fond of me, Verity thought with surprise.

Charlotte had further surprised her by promising a quiet evening at home.

But no sooner was supper over and they were seated over the tea tray in the drawing room than Charlotte handed Verity the Duke of Denbigh's letter. "So you see how clever you are," cried Charlotte. "Do pen something to show him that he would be better off in London."

"When did this arrive?" Verity asked quietly.

"This morning," said Charlotte, avoiding her eyes.

"I see," Verity said sadly.

Charlotte would remain fond of her only for so long as she proved useful. Verity thought again about leaving and then decided to oblige Charlotte with one more letter.

The next day, when Verity, accompanied by James, had gone out to exercise the pets, Charlotte crept quietly into Verity's room and searched through her belongings until she found Verity's money. She scooped it all up and took it away.

When Verity returned and found her money missing, the alarm was raised. Charlotte cheerfully tried to blame the servants, but Verity could not bring herself to allow that. She had a very shrewd idea that Charlotte had taken the money herself. She sat down and wrote a letter to her father, explaining that her money had been stolen and begging for more.

James was taking the letters to the post when Charlotte hailed him. "I am going out, James," she said. "Hand me the letters and I will take them."

James passed them over. Charlotte waited until she was in her carriage with her maid and then scanned the letters. She gently extracted the one addressed to Mr. Bascombe and crushed it in her hand when her maid was not looking. The one to the Duke of Denbigh she took to the post.

Unknown to Charlotte, by the end of a bare three weeks in London, Verity had become very well known. She was a familiar figure in Hyde Park, with her entourage of strange pets. Tray, the French greyhound, was slowly dwindling to a correct size and ran in circles in the park, barking with delight. Peter, the cat, was glossy and sleek. Above them sailed the great parrot, alighting occasionally on the back of the bench on which Verity sat. The elderly Dowager Countess of Wythe had taken a fancy to Verity and her pets and often sat with her on the park bench for part of the afternoon, if the day was fine. Lady Wythe was as slim and straight as a young girl although she was in her sixties. Her puckered and wrinkled crab-apple skin was heavily painted and rouged. Her back was ramrod-straight and she was proud of boasting that never once had it come into contact with the back of a chair. She detested the latest fashion of "lounging," damning it as decadent. But apart from her occasionally acid tongue and her obvious dislike of Verity's hostess, she was an amusing companion. It also transpired that she knew the Duke of Denbigh.

"Tell me all you know about him," asked Verity eagerly.

The countess rolled one pale blue eye in Verity's direction. "Aha! You have joined the ranks of ladies eager to grasp the title. No. Wait a bit. I have it! You say you are a country lawyer's daughter with a negligible dowry, or rather, negligible by society's standards. You have too much good sense to fly so high, but Mrs. Manners has not. It is said he proposed to her once and was turned down for lack of the ready. She hopes to try her luck with him and wishes you to aid her."

Verity spread her hands in a deprecating way but did not reply.

"And since Mrs. Manners has no use for her own sex—unless they prove to be of some use to her—she will put an end to your London jaunt very quickly if you do not do something to help. Am I right?"

"I wonder where that parrot has disappeared to?" said Verity, scanning the sky.

"In other words, you will not discuss your hostess," said the countess. "And very correct, too. I shall help you nonetheless, for I enjoy your company and wish more of it. Denbigh. Let me see. Devilishly handsome, and such legs." The countess kissed her gloved fingertips. "He has a good, strong face, but is a trifle cynical about the mouth. His hair is pure gold and curls naturally. He is clever. You must wonder what a clever man was doing to propose to Mrs. Manners. But remember, he was twenty-four and had not been in love, or so I imagine. At that time, Mrs. Manners was being sponsored by her aunt, Lady Phillips. Now Lady Phillips was a high stickler if ever there was one. She told Charlotte—and in my hearing, mark you, for we were wont to take tea together—that she must keep her mouth shut at all times and confine her remarks to yes and no. Which she did. She had that dewy, untouched look that yet contained a hidden fire. It would have taken a very old and shrewd man to have guessed that the fires that lurked beneath her delectable bosom were the fires of ambition and frustration—frustration at having to keep her pretty mouth shut, don't you see. So Denbigh was bewitched. Every man who saw her was bewitched. She did not have a very large dowry and she had a passion for French dressmakers. Manners may have guessed her secret. He was in trade, you know, and was a sharp businessman, and so it is possible he was better able to recognize cupidity when he came across it than Denbigh. He showered her with expensive presents, jeweled clockwork, nightingales, and the like. Lady Phillips sent them back. But clever Charlotte bribed her maid to collect them and hide them.

"And so they were married, she and Manners." The countess sighed and poked at the grass at her feet with the pointed end of her parasol. "Denbigh was most upset, you know. But it couldn't have lasted very long—his upset, I mean. For I know he met her at a ball three months after she married Manners, and of course, don't you see, she was talking to beat the band. It wasn't that she was *particularly* silly—not more than most—but Denbigh, I should judge, had dreamed of a fount of wit and intelligence. Odd man. He likes intelligent women. It must be about the only thing about him that is unfashionable."

"Now he can marry whom he pleases," said Verity, half to herself.

"Even the daughter of a country lawyer?"

"No, my lady, and I know you are teasing me. I am fortunate in that I have no need to marry. We are comfortably off and I keep house for Papa."

"Very sensible," said the countess, staring straight ahead as she always did. Naturally, she considered screwing your head around to speak to the person next to you vulgar in the extreme. "When poor Wythe was taken, I found to my sur-

36

prise that I was beginning to enjoy myself for the first time in my life. Such a pity I was too old to take a lover."

"My lady!"

"Your generation is so mealy-mouthed."

Verity returned to Charlotte and told her that she, Verity, had learned that the duke favored intelligent women. "So perhaps you could hire a tutor, dear Charlotte, and learn to discuss all the clever things that will impress him."

Charlotte laughed and laughed at that. "You poor, dearest bumpkin," she said at last, drying her eyes. "With beauty such as mine, I do not even need to open a book. Once he sees me, his defenses will collapse. But write your clever letters to lure him to London."

When Verity had left the room, Charlotte looked at the parrot and shrugged. "Why keep a dog and bark yourself?"

Chapter Three

The Duke of Denbigh picked up the latest Verity-Charlotte letter and took it out to the walled garden to read. The splendid weather had broken and although the day was sunny, it was also blustery and cold. The walled garden was one of his favorite retreats. He sat on a low stone bench at the south end where a peach tree, espaliered against the wall, turned its glossy leaves up to the sun.

The high walls cut off the wind. The air was redolent of the fragrant smell of herbs, vegetables, and rich earth.

He had replied to her letter about Kean's performance with a reminiscence of having seen Mrs. Siddons in Monk Lewis's melodrama, *Veroni, or The Novice of St. Marks*.

He opened the letter eagerly. Charlotte had apparently met Monk Lewis.

Matthew Gregory Lewis had been a twenty-year-old junior attaché working in The Hague when, inspired by the novels of Mrs. Radcliffe, he had written *The Monk*. It was at once attacked for vice and immorality by the critics, and that had ensured

its success and gained the author his new name of
Monk Lewis.

Verity had written:

*I confess I was very excited when I set out
for Mrs. Abernethy's in Montagu Street. We
were to dine at seven, very fashionable. When
we crossed Oxford Street, I could not help
thinking that I would never get used to such a
glittering sight as this famous place. Until
eleven o'clock in the evening, it is as crowded
as any fair. The long line of oil lamps down
the center made it look on this misty night
like some gigantic necklace. Come, my dear
recluse, you must admit there is truth in Dr.
Johnson's remark that a man who is tired of
London is tired of life.*

*But to return to my muttons. There I was,
trembling in the carriage at the thought of
being so soon in the presence of the famous
Mr. Monk Lewis. I imagined him as tall and
gaunt and sinister and dressed all in black.
His voice would be hollow, as if sounding
from the inside of a marble tomb.*

*Imagine my surprise to find Mr. Lewis was
an odd-looking little man with a strangely
boyish appearance, although he is quite old—
thirty-something, I believe. He had queerish
eyes, protruding, and like the eyes one sees on
certain insects. He did not say anything very
extraordinary although I only overheard a
little of his conversation. He is not in the
slightest interested in the ladies, you see, and
shuns them. Mrs. Abernethy is a great
favorite of his, however, and perhaps the only
lady who is! It is said his chambers in
Albany are cluttered with bric-a-brac and*

*precious objects and that there are mirrors
everywhere. It is rumored Lord Byron went to
one of his parties and swore never to go
again. He is reported to have said, "I never
will dine with a middle-aged man who fills
up his tables with young ensigns and has
looking-glass panels to his bookcases."*

*The inclement weather means I have not
seen quite as much of my dear Lady Wythe as
I would wish. So when I take my oddity of
pets to the park, I find I miss her very much.
She has a sharp wit and yet has a generous
spirit.*

The duke put down the letter and stared unsee-
ingly across the pleasant garden. The letter was,
in its way, the sort of gossipy letter he would have
expected Charlotte to write. And yet a Charlotte
who quoted Dr. Johnson did not tally with the image he had of her. But seven years had passed and
so she had probably matured. He had misjudged
her. She had probably loved Manners and her grief
over his death had made her turn her mind to less
frivolous ideas. He picked up the letter again.

The letter went on to describe the wonders of the
new gas lamps in parts of Pall Mall and White-
cross Street and how strange it was to stand under
such a blaze of light instead of feeling one's way
under the weak lights of the parish lamps, which
were always blowing out. But it was the ending of
the letter that really startled the duke.

*I went, with great trepidation, accompanied
by Lady Wythe, to Euston to take a ride in
Mr. Trevithick's Catch-me-who-can. It cost a
shilling and we went round and round at*

fifteen miles an hour. Mr. Trevithick has
evidently invented a steam boiler, which can
work to a pressure of one hundred pounds.
Lady Wythe said the speed was indecent and
would cause damage to the brains of the
already weak-minded, but I pointed out that
the mail coaches reached that speed and my
lady said that must explain why there were so
many totty-headed young men about London,
for they will ride on the roof of the mail coach
and bribe the coachmen to let them take the
reins.

The duke tried to imagine Charlotte being interested in any piece of machinery and found he could
not. Perhaps the pleasures of the Season had
changed. There was no mention of balls, ridottos,
drums, or routs.

But he could not leave his estates. There was
much to be done.

Verity sat at her desk over a blank sheet of paper. She had been to Almack's with Charlotte the
evening before and wondered if the duke would
appreciate a description of that. But then, he knew
Almack's famous assembly rooms in King Street
very well. It was pointless to ask Charlotte for
help, for Charlotte always shrugged and told her
to write something amusing. Charlotte had even
given up reading Verity's letters although she
waited eagerly for the duke's replies, not because
of the content of the letters but always to see if he
would say something about coming to London.

At Almack's, there had been a great deal of gossip
about the duke. Several young ladies had talked
their parents into driving them to the duke's es-

tates and staging a carriage accident outside his
gates. But in each case, the families had been
taken to the house and courteously entertained by
the housekeeper while the carriage was swiftly
mended. The duke had not put in an appearance.
People were beginning to say he had become a
recluse.

Charlotte came in and put a letter from Denbigh
down in front of Verity. "You can read it," said
Charlotte, yawning, for she had lately risen and
was still in her nightdress.

Verity looked surprised. Usually Charlotte
ripped open Denbigh's letters as soon as they arrived.

"I have lost interest," said Charlotte, slumping
down inelegantly in a spoon-back chair by the window. "It may have escaped your notice, since you
have been jauntering around London with that old
fright, Lady Wythe—how did you persuade such a
tartar to take you anywhere so unfashionable as
the Tower?—that the Earl of Veney has been court-
ing me."

"No, I had noticed," said Verity cautiously. "He
is a trifle old for you, Charlotte, is he not?"

"He is forty-five—no great age. He is an earl and
very rich. Veney is considered a great catch. All are
jealous of me."

"I am sure they are," said Verity, ever diplo-
matic.

"So there is no need for you to go on writing to
Denbigh. I have decided to accept Veney."

"Very well," said Verity, feeling depressed. Then
she realized her usefulness to Charlotte was over,
but Mr. Bascombe was still in Scotland and the
house was shut up. "When do you wish me to return home, Charlotte?"

"Oh, no need for that," said Charlotte airily. "I

am very fond of you, Verity. I thought you knew that."

Charlotte believed she spoke the truth, but the truth was that Verity had become very popular with society and Lord Veney had said that he knew Mrs. Manners to be an exceptional lady to have such an intelligent and pleasant companion. "You can always tell a lady by the company she keeps," he had added sententiously. Lord Veney always said things like that. It was as if he felt pompous statements offset the lechery in his soul.

Charlotte was convinced that any man who showed an interest in Verity was merely cultivating her friendship so as to get closer to her mistress. She had fallen into the habit of referring to Verity as her companion.

"When do you think he will propose?" asked Verity.

"This week, I think. He is already champing at the bit. But there are going to be no more proposals in the drawing room. The Yellow Saloon has just been redecorated. Pomfret will make sure no one goes near it but Lord Veney. The drawing room has long windows leading into that excuse for a garden at the back. I am persuaded some vicious female came by that way and poured poison into Chalfont's ears. Chalfont, by the way, is gone from town, so you will not be able to question him. Fiddle. I go driving with Veney this afternoon, so I shan't need you."

When she had gone, Verity slowly opened the letter.

Dear Mrs. Manners,

There is no longer reason for me to come to London, for I can live there through your vivid descriptions.

43

Now, I know he is teasing, but Charlotte would not, thought Verity. The duke went on to give a detailed description of the work on his estates, his impatience with his tenant farmers who fought against using any of the new phosphates to enrich the land, and his battle with the local magistrates who would insist on cruel punishments for poachers. It was quite a long letter and ended with the hope of receiving further news from Charlotte.

I am become spoiled by your letters, and find my magazines and newspapers tedious in comparison.

But I cannot write any more, thought Verity. In her mind's eye, she had made the duke look like that gentleman in the posting house she had seen so long ago. She had no money to pay postage herself. She could write a letter and leave it on the hall table where it would be dealt with along with the rest of the post, but Charlotte might see it. Verity hated not having any money at all. The trip on the Catch-me-who-can had cost a shilling and Lady Wythe had paid that. Verity wondered again whether Charlotte had taken her money.

When she had told Lady Wythe of her loss, the dowager had immediately suggested that Charlotte had done it in order to keep her until her usefulness ran out.

Verity spent a comfortable hour in the park with her old friend but could not tell her about the letters, for Verity felt that would be betraying her hostess.

The weather continued cold. Verity shivered indoors. Charlotte was parsimonious about things like fires. She never seemed to feel the cold herself and moved through the chilly rooms of her mansion dressed in the thinnest of muslin.

Lord Veney was to call to ask for Charlotte's hand in marriage the next day. As she had no parents to approach, she assumed that was his intent. "And after what he did to me at the back of the opera box," said Charlotte, her face flushing, "then he had better."

"What did he do?" asked Verity.

"When you were leaning over the box with a hand to your ear to catch every note, he stole a kiss."

"Was that so very bad?"

"Wait. Then he plunged his hand down the front of my gown and tweaked my breast!"

"Was he foxed? I mean, why would a gentleman do a thing like that?"

Charlotte gave Verity an odd look. "You'll find out one day," she said. "Now, the earl is a bit of a rip, so I must dress accordingly. There is no need for you to be present."

"Charlotte, you will be spending the rest of your life with this man. Do you have affection and respect for him?"

"Affection and respect for Veney? You odd girl. I tell you straight, he is a boor and a lecher. But once I am countess, he may find his pleasures elsewhere. After I breed, I shall be finished with that side of marriage—and let us hope he can manage it quickly, for I could not bear him in my bed for very long."

Pretty Polly wheezed and rattled the bars of its cage. "And keep that smelly parrot locked up while he is here," said Charlotte, getting up and leaving the room.

Verity went over to the toilet table, filled a basin with water, and bathed her hot cheeks. Charlotte often sounded like a strumpet.

It appeared she was determined to dress like one for the proposal.

That evening, she gave Verity a dress rehearsal, parading before her in a morning gown of pink spotted muslin. It was simple and correct in line, with little puff sleeves stiffened with cambric and with three deep flounces at the hem. But the muslin was nearly transparent and Charlotte had damped it so that it clung to her body.

"I can see your garters through the cloth," said Verity faintly.

"Good," said Charlotte. "That should fetch him."

Just before Lord Veney was due to arrive, Verity locked Pretty Polly up in its great brass cage, removed the cat and dog from her bed for the umpteenth time by yanking the coverlet and sending them tumbling onto the floor, and went down the back stairs to the kitchens to discuss arrangements for an engagement celebration with the housekeeper.

Verity liked going down to the kitchens and sitting at the scrubbed table and talking to the housekeeper, Mrs. Andrew.

Upstairs in Verity's bedroom, Pretty Polly was throwing a parrot tantrum, jumping up and down in its cage. At last it settled down on the bottom, its shoulders hunched. It cast a bleak eye at the door of the cage and then hopped two steps and eased its right claw through the bars. It fiddled with the catch. There was a click and the door sprang open. Pretty Polly shuffled out onto the perch outside. It heard a sound at the door and hopped down to the floor and leaned against the wall.

Two chambermaids came in to clean Verity's room. The parrot shuffled through the open door, unobserved by them. It made its way to the main staircase and cocked its head to one side. The parrot raised a claw and gave its head feathers a meditative scratch; then it combed out the gold fringe on its legs with its beak and began to hop down the stairs.

The double doors to the Yellow Saloon were standing open. There was a large bowl of nuts on a console table in the center of the room.

Pretty Polly hopped onto the table, selected a large walnut, and retreated behind a china cabinet in the corner to crack the shell.

Lord Veney was late. Charlotte had damped her muslin for the third time when he eventually arrived.

Obeying his instructions to the letter, Pomfret showed the earl into the saloon, served him a glass of canary, bowed, and left.

With his glass in his hand, Lord Veney strutted up and down the long room, picking up objects and examining them and then putting them down. There was a carved box on a little side table. He opened the lid and it immediately began to crank out a tune. "Music boxes," said Lord Veney aloud, and shut the lid with a snap. "Never could abide the bloody things."

"Pretty Polly," said a voice from behind the china cabinet.

Lord Veney stood amazed, his glass raised halfway to his lips.

Then the voice began again and it was undoubtedly Charlotte's voice, "Affection and respect for Veney? You odd girl. I tell you straight, he is a boor and a lecher. But once I am countess, he may find his pleasures elsewhere. After I breed, I shall be finished with that side of marriage—and let us hope he can manage it quickly, for I could not bear him in my bed for very long."

Lord Veney carefully put down his glass and looked at the empty fireplace. He was sure the flue was acting as some sort of speaking tube and that what he had just heard was Charlotte talking to Verity in a room above.

He thought of plain and dowdy Miss Tring of Gloucester, who had adored him for years and whom he had snubbed. And all because of an infatuation for some trollop. Miss Tring should break her heart no longer. He would ride to Gloucester that very day and propose.

The doors of the saloon opened and Charlotte tripped in. Lord Veney looked her up and down. "You are disgusting and shameless," he said.

He walked past her. He did not even stop to collect his hat and cane. He went straight out of the house and soon his angry voice could be heard shouting to his coachmen to "spring 'em."

Charlotte began to scream, and when she had finished screaming, she demanded that every inch of the room be searched. Pretty Polly had sidled quietly out as the street door was slammed by Lord Veney. The parrot sailed quietly up the stairs. The chambermaids had finished their work and the bedroom door was standing open. The parrot flew back to its cage, and by the time Verity had coaxed the distraught Charlotte up to her room, the bird was asleep.

Freezing rooms and wet muslin finally got the better of Charlotte's robust constitution and she came down with a feverish cold. Verity nursed her conscientiously, glad that none of the pets showed any inclination to invade Charlotte's bedchamber.

The Duke of Denbigh had hired a new secretary. Unlike his father, he believed in employing local people whenever possible. The secretary was, therefore, Mr. Tom Crabbe, a local youth who had excelled at the village school. He was correct, hardworking, and obedient. But the duke was wondering whether he had made a mistake. The letters from Charlotte had ceased. He had broken down and written a teasing request for more news, but still nothing arrived from London. He began to suspect his poor secretary of losing letters. The duke started to collect all the post himself. Still no letter. His days began to take on a new pattern. The post boy arrived at ten in the morning. The duke rose at six. From six to ten, life seemed full of anticipation and promise; from ten to sunset, it seemed like a desert.

He began to become angry. He felt as if Charlotte had rejected and betrayed him again. At last his anger was so great that he decided he had been right not to go to London to see her. She had not changed one whit.

Recovered from her fever, Charlotte smiled wanly at Verity. "The next man who means to propose to me can do so outside this house. There is a curse on it."

Verity, who did not believe in curses but did believe that Charlotte was unfortunate in her choice of suitors, remained silent.

"You are a good and kind friend, Verity," said Charlotte, stretching out her plump little hand and

49

clasping Verity's strong, slim one. "Has Denbigh written?"

"You told me to stop writing to him, if you remember. He did write some time ago, obviously wondering at your silence."

Charlotte dropped Verity's hand and stared at her in amazement. "You utter fool," she snapped. "What else had you to do with your time?"

Verity held her gaze. "I was nursing you, among other things."

Charlotte shifted restlessly against the pillows. "Yes, yes. I am grateful. Very. But you should have used your wits, girl. With Veney off, then it follows that Denbigh must be on again."

Verity sighed. Why had her father decided to stay in Edinburgh? Aloud she said, "I might have taken the initiative, but I do not have any money, if you will recall, not even for a stamp."

"Oh, that. It is your own fault, you know, I do not know why you persisted in stopping me from investigating the servants."

"Do you not?" asked Verity quietly.

Charlotte shifted again. "You have only to ask me for money. I shall let you have some . . . er, tomorrow. Please be my angelest darling and write to Denbigh."

The Duke of Denbigh looked at the letter as if it were a snake. To leave it unread and forget about the whole business would mean he would keep his peace of mind. It lay unopened for the whole day until curiosity overcame him.

He read it with surprise and consternation. Charlotte had been ill! That was why she had ceased to write. And he had credited her with all sorts of evil machinations.

He sat down and began to write.

Charlotte looked up as Verity quietly entered her bedchamber with the post. "A letter from Denbigh."

"You read it," said Charlotte petulantly. "He is probably boring on about crops as usual."

Verity broke open the heavy seal. The letter was short. The duke was alarmed to hear of her illness. He was traveling to London to see her and would arrive at his town house in Cavendish Square at the end of the week.

"Huzzah!" cried Charlotte, her face flushed with excitement. She flung back the covers, jumped from the bed, ran to the door, and started to shout for Pomfret.

Verity remained with the letter in her hand. She felt very sad. The dream was over. She had fondly imagined continuing the correspondence for a few more weeks until her return home, a few more weeks of dreaming of this fantasy lover.

She got to her feet and began to open all the drawers in the bureau in the corner of Charlotte's room. There, stuffed at the very back of the bottom drawer, she found her purse. She was not very surprised. She stood, weighing it up and down in her hand. Why retreat now? Life was very pleasant. Charlotte was bearable. If she journeyed to Market Basset, she would need to stay with one of the neighbors until her father's return. She could not leave the pets to Charlotte's tender mercies, and she could not think of one sober citizen in her hometown who would be prepared to put up with the menagerie. Besides, why not stay and see this duke? He could not possibly be such a paragon as Lady Wythe had described. He was thirty-one and not yet married. Probably this Adonis was very difficult. His letters had been informative and charming. Verity suddenly giggled. How amusing it would be if it transpired he had not written any of them and had got a friend to write them for him.

Having decided to stay until her father sent for her, Verity made up her mind to do some shopping for herself. She could now afford to be a little extravagant.

She returned later that day, happy and exhausted. She had bought a new collar for Tray, a toy mouse for the cat, hothouse grapes for the parrot, and a length of burgundy-colored silk for herself. Pastels did not become Verity. Of course, she was not going to all this trouble for the duke, she told herself firmly. She simply felt she would be cheered by a new gown.

Charlotte spent the remaining days before the duke's arrival in a flurry of hectic activity. The house was full from morning to night with mantua makers, milliners, jewelers, and plumassiers.

Verity diligently stitched at her new gown or walked the pets in the park. "Mrs. Manners is in high alt," Verity confided in Lady Wythe. "Denbigh is coming to town expressly to see her."

"And what," said Lady Wythe, looking at the parrot who was stalking up and down in front of the bench on which they sat, its head bowed like an anxious old lawyer, "will Denbigh think when, instead of meeting the authoress of all these charming letters, he meets Mrs. Manners?"

"I do not know what you mean," said Verity.

"Oh, yes, you do," said the countess. "I only wish I could be there to see the fun. Here comes Mr. George Wilson to talk to you. A good prospect, if you are interested. He has a comfortable fortune and is not ill-favored. The only drawback is that he lives with his widowed mother."

"And why should that be a drawback?"

" 'Tis said she is determined to be the only female in the Wilson household. I have no patience with such selfishness."

Verity experienced a qualm of conscience. Did her father really want to marry? And was her own single state what was preventing him from doing so?

She smiled with more warmth than usual at Mr. Wilson as he approached. He was a pleasant-looking man. He had only two pockmarks on his face and his brown hair was thick and springy. He was soberly but fashionably dressed. His legs were a trifle bowed.

"I tried to call on you yesterday," began Mr. Wilson, "but I was told that you were not at home to anyone."

"It is Mrs. Manners who is not at home at present," said Verity. "She is expecting an important visitor at the weekend."

"And who is that?"

Verity saw no reason to keep the duke's visit a secret. "Denbigh," she said.

"Our new duke? That will put more hearts than Mrs. Manners's in a flutter. But not yours, I trust, Miss Bascombe?"

"Now, how can I get in a flutter about a man I have never seen," teased Verity.

"Oh, Denbigh is very dashing. Quite the heart-breaker," said Mr. Wilson gloomily. "Will you walk with me a little, Miss Bascombe? That is, if you will excuse us, Lady Wythe."

Lady Wythe inclined her head gracefully. "Go ahead, Miss Bascombe," she said. "I shall watch your creatures for you."

Verity walked sedately with Mr. Wilson. He was a thoroughly worthy gentleman, she thought. Perhaps love was something you really had to work at. Perhaps all the books and poems lied. For she had seen no man in London to stir her feelings even in the slightest.

Chapter Four

The Duke of Denbigh's town house turned a blank, unscalable wall to Cavendish Square. Like many of the aristocracy, his father had opted for a fortresslike appearance outside and kept all the elegance and grandeur for the inside.

The present duke had toyed with the idea of having the wall torn down. It had been built originally to protect the house and its inmates from the mobs that had thronged Oxford Street on the road to Tyburn on hanging days. But now the hangings were outside Newgate, and Oxford Street had become respectable.

But as Denbigh viewed the square, it looked so much like the same bleak square he had hated as a little boy that he decided to let the wall stand. Looking over the railings of the square as his carriage turned into it, he saw the sooty black trees still surrounding the dreary grass plot in the center with the equestrian statue of the Duke of Cumberland, "Butcher" Cumberland who had massacred so many of the Scotch. A few miserable governesses, huddled in shawls against the biting wind, shepherded wan-faced schoolboys round and round for their daily constitutional. Like a prison yard, thought the duke.

Behind him came carriage after carriage bearing his staff. The town house had been kept by a caretaker and his wife, as his father had not used it in years and the duke himself had not been there since he was a boy. There had been no time to send the servants in advance to make things ready.

He entered and walked slowly through the silent, enormous rooms. In a saloon on the first floor, the chandeliers hung shrouded in their Holland bags, and the long looking glasses at either end of the room made it seem even more enormous.

He could hear his servants' muttered exclamations of dismay. But the caretaker was old and infirm and could not be expected to prepare the mansion with only the help of his equally aged wife. The duke had not realized until his arrival how old and infirm the man was. Time to give him a generous pension and retire him.

Soon a fire was blazing in the library to dispel the chill. He stood in front of it and thought of Charlotte Manners. Now that he was in London, now that he could see her any time he liked, he felt he had been too precipitate. He would hold an impromptu party in two or three days' time, some cards and music and supper, and invite her to that.

All Saturday, Charlotte waited in a fever of excitement, running to the window every time she heard the sound of a horse or a carriage. She had changed her gown five times by late afternoon.

"What has happened?" she asked Verity for what seemed the hundredth time.

"Perhaps he has been delayed on the road," said Verity, smoothing down the folds of her burgundy silk gown with a nervous hand. "Perhaps it might be an idea to send one of the footmen around to Cavendish Square just to look, you know. The house has a very high wall in front of it, but if the duke has arrived, there should be a great deal of coming and going."

Charlotte rang the bell and ordered Pomfret to send a footman immediately to Cavendish Square.

The day was turning dark and a thin, greasy drizzle had begun to fall. Verity wandered over to the window and looked out at the dripping plane trees in the square. A lamplighter was going on his rounds with his ladder and can of whale oil. Soon the lights of Berkeley Square began to flicker in the increasing gloom. Verity shivered. The drawing room was very cold.

"It might be an idea to light a fire in here," she suggested. "You are but recently recovered, Charlotte, and also, when the duke arrives, he would perhaps be cheered by the sight of a welcoming blaze."

Charlotte nodded and ordered a fire to be made up. Verity sighed with relief. She did not want to put a shawl over her splendid gown. After all, she had gone to such trouble to make it that it would be a pity if the duke did not see it.

James, the second footman, returned with the intelligence that the duke had indeed arrived. There were lights in all the rooms in the upper storeys of the mansion.

"It is six o'clock," said Verity. "He will not call now."

"He must!" said Charlotte furiously. The greyhound trotted in front of her and she lashed out at the animal with her foot. She missed it, but Tray cowered and fled to the shelter of Verity's skirts.

There came a brisk knocking at the street door.

Charlotte ran to a chair by the fire and arranged herself gracefully.

Both ladies waited anxiously. Then Pomfret came in with a letter, which he handed to Charlotte. She recognized Denbigh's seal and tore it open. Verity found she was holding her breath.

"Fiddle!" said Charlotte furiously. "He has invited me to a small party on Tuesday evening. That means I shall not have the advantage over anyone else. I should have read those letters you sent, Verity. You obviously did a bad job."

Verity kept her temper with an effort. "You turned him down once. The fact that he has invited you at all is a credit to my skill."

"So you say," commented Charlotte nastily. "And as you are not included in the invitation, you cannot go. *Such* a pity after all the effort you went to to make that gown!"

Verity went up to her room in a fury. "I don't care," she said aloud. "I simply don't care. It has nothing to do with me. I must write to Papa and get him to give me a firm date for his return."

But when she went to bed that night and felt two thumps as the dog and cat leaped in beside her, she did not shoo them off. Tray was pressed on one side of her and Peter, the cat, on the other. Pretty Polly shuffled up and down on the bed head before falling asleep.

Verity felt a rush of affection for these pets of Charlotte's. At least someone likes me, she thought, before turning over and going to sleep.

When Charlotte entered the state saloons on the first floor of the duke's mansion on Tuesday and surveyed the assembled guests, her heart sank right down to her sky-blue kid slippers. The other people invited seemed to consist of all of London's most aged and highest sticklers, and, oh, dear, there was that old fright, Lady Wythe, sitting by the fire and lookingly wickedly amused about something.

Charlotte was wearing a very pretty sky-blue muslin gown. She saw her reflection in one of the long looking glasses and frowned. She was wearing six ostrich plumes in her hair, all dyed sky-blue to match her gown. Verity had suggested the effect was a trifle top-heavy, and Charlotte had replied by saying, "What does a provincial little nobody know about fashion?" But the feathers *did* look ridiculous. Then Charlotte realized that since she had begun to take Verity everywhere with her, Verity's very presence assured her, Charlotte, of a warm welcome. There was something about Verity that seemed to melt the heart of the flintiest dowager.

The duke had been talking to Mr. and Mrs. Hatfield, an elderly couple whom Charlotte had once snubbed. He turned, saw Charlotte, and smiled.

Charlotte felt as if all the breath had been knocked out of her body. She had forgotten he was so very handsome. He was wearing a black evening coat, and his black pantaloons were molded to his muscled legs to just above his ankles. He was wearing green-and-gold-striped silk stockings and flat black shoes.

He crossed immediately to Charlotte's side and stood smiling down at her. He raised her hand to his lips. "I trust you are recovered from your illness, Mrs. Manners?" he asked.

"Yes, thank you," said Charlotte, blushing adorably and looking down at her feet.

"I must thank you," he went on, "for your charming and delightful letters."

"Thank you," mumbled Charlotte, unusually tongue-tied.

"And how are Tray and Peter and that parrot with the ridiculous name?"

With an effort, Charlotte realized he was talking about her pets.

"Tiresome as usual," she said.

He laughed and Charlotte wondered what she had said that was so amusing. "You cannot fool me, Mrs. Manners," he said. "I know from your letters that you quite dote on them."

She raised her eyes fleetingly to his, and he saw with surprise the brief flash of shock followed by irritation in them. Charlotte was thinking, Damn, Verity, why did she have to drivel on about that useless zoo?

She contented herself by saying, "Mmm," and then added brightly, "Now that you are in town, Denbigh, you must agree it is a vastly more interesting place than the country."

"It has certain attractions, I agree," he murmured, and Charlotte gave him a flirtatious look and raised her fan to her face. "I was interested in your description of your meeting with Monk Lewis."

"Oh, that," said Charlotte, remembering that tedious evening with dismay. What would Verity have written? Verity was a bit of a bluestocking. She must have enthused like mad. "Yes, he is a divinely interesting man," Charlotte went on. "Those piercing eyes, that noble forehead."

"You have certainly changed your views," said the duke. "As I recall, you thought he had eyes like those of an insect."

Charlotte laughed, that tinkling laugh she had practiced so often. She rapped him playfully on the shoulder with her fan. "Oh, you must allow us ladies to change our minds," she said.

60

At that moment, the Countess of Wythe rose from her seat by the fire and came to join them.

"I do not see Miss Bascombe," she said.

Charlotte looked at the countess with dislike. "Miss Bascombe was not invited," she said.

"Who is Miss Bascombe?" asked the duke.

"She is a lady who went to the same Bath seminary as I," said Charlotte. "She is not very good *ton*, a country lawyer's daughter, but I felt it would do the poor thing good to have some fun."

"I am a friend of Miss Bascombe," said the dowager. "A most entertaining lady. She has become quite a feature in Hyde Park when she walks along with her dog, cat, and parrot."

"*My* dog, cat, and parrot," Charlotte said between her teeth.

"Of course." The countess gave a crocodile smile. "But the creatures are so devoted to Miss Bascombe, and she to them, that I had quite forgotten."

Then Lady Wythe looked brightly from the duke's puzzled face to Charlotte's furious one, with her head cocked to one side like a bird looking for worms.

"Do walk with me a little, Your Grace," said Charlotte, now desperate to get away from the dowager.

He bowed to Lady Wythe and held out his arm courteously to Charlotte. "I am so glad there is to be dancing," said Charlotte, peeping up at him. "I long to dance."

"Alas, I had meant to have dancing," said the duke ruefully. "But I had not realized I had asked so many elderly people. I am afraid it is going to be an evening of cards and gossip."

Charlotte saw they were approaching Mr. and Mrs. Hatfield and tugged a little at the duke's arm to turn him about, but he bowed to the Hatfields and came to a stop. He glanced down at Charlotte in surprise and irritation. She should have curtsied to the Hatfields, but she stood unmoving, possessively holding on to his arm.

As if to highlight Charlotte's lack of manners, Mrs. Hatfield sank into a deep court curtsy and Mr. Hatfield gave a magnificent bow punctuated with many wavings of his handkerchief and a long scrape of his foot along the floor.

The duke bowed low in return, and there was nothing else Charlotte could do but release his arm and drop a curtsy.

"You promised us cards, Denbigh," said Mr. Hatfield.

"And you shall have them," the duke replied. "The tables are already set up in the adjoining room." He turned and announced that the card playing was about to begin. In the general push to the card room, Charlotte was jostled aside and ended up making up a foursome at whist with a tall colonel, his wife, and a thin, faded spinster.

Charlotte always cheated at cards. Since she usually played cards only with adoring young men, she got away with it. But the spinster called Miss Jessop exclaimed in a strident voice, "You are cheating, Mrs. Manners, and it will not do."

So the mortified Charlotte lost a great deal of money.

The card game dragged on for what seemed an eternity and Charlotte could hardly believe her ordeal had come to an end when supper was announced.

She stood up hopefully, looking toward the duke. But he was escorting Lady Wythe, who was the most senior in rank of the ladies. Charlotte was placed somewhere down near the end of the table.

She felt a lump rising in her throat. No one

seemed to think she was pretty. She picked at her food and drank a great deal too much. At long last Lady Wythe rose, signaling that the ladies were to retire to the drawing room and leave the gentlemen to their wine.

So Charlotte sat in the drawing room and waited and waited, while all about her the ladies conversed. She missed Verity dreadfully. Verity seemed to have an endless fund of small talk, and Charlotte had become used to never having to make much of an effort herself.

At last, after an hour, the gentlemen came in. Mrs. Hatfield entertained the company with a pianoforte recital, so there was no chance for Charlotte to talk to the duke. Then when that was finished, Miss Jessop sang some very long ballads.

At last Charlotte was urged to entertain the company by some of the ladies who, though Charlotte did not know it, were beginning to feel sorry for her because she looked so lost and miserable.

Charlotte sat down at the piano and hammered out that piece called "The Woodpecker," which every young miss was forced to learn at some time or another. The applause was warm and polite. The duke crossed to the piano to thank her and Charlotte gave him a blinding smile.

He smiled warmly back, quite enchanted with her. She was more beautiful than he had remembered. He was heartily sorry he had just invited the first names that had come into his head. How depressing it must be for her not to have any young people to talk to.

"You did not mention Miss Bascombe in your letters," he said, "or I would have included her in the invitation."

"Perhaps if you care to call, you can meet her. She is quite amusing in a provincial kind of way."

The smile left his eyes. The Charlotte who had written those letters could not be the Charlotte who called her friends "provincial."

But, he reflected, it would do no harm to take Mrs. Manners out driving. He was sure, away from social strains and stresses, she would turn into that lady who had become his favorite correspondent.

"May I take you driving tomorrow?" he asked. "Provided, of course, that the weather is not too bad."

"I should like that above all things," Charlotte was about to say, but she was shrewd in the ways of stalking a man and so she affected disappointment instead. "What a pity, Denbigh. I am already engaged to go out driving."

The duke's interest in her quickened even more. Of course she would have many beaux. "Then the day after," he said eagerly.

He watched anxiously as Charlotte pretended to sort through the busy appointment book of her mind. Then her face cleared. "That would be splendid."

"Shall we say four-thirty?"

"Yes, four-thirty."

Later that night, Charlotte sat on the end of Verity's bed and listened, appalled, as that young lady recited all of the things she had written to the duke about.

"A visit to the Tower . . . and a ride on the Catch-me-who-can? How could you, Verity? That is the behavior of a rustic."

Verity flushed with annoyance. "My yokelism does not seem to have prevented him from enjoying my letters."

"If only you had had the wit to write them more like *me* and less like you!"

64

"If I had written them like *you*, they wouldn't have fetched him," said Verity tartly.

Charlotte was about to say something very nasty. But the thought that the evening she had just spent would have been so much more pleasurable had Verity been there to protect her from the dragons stopped her.

"Now you are furious with me," she said instead. "Dear Verity, give me a smile. We are friends, are we not?"

Verity looked at Charlotte's pleading blue eyes. No one was completely selfish and Charlotte did really seem to want to be friends.

"Of course we are," said Verity, stretching out her hand. Charlotte took it and gave it a squeeze. Verity was such a good foil. No beauty there, so no competition. Yes, Verity could be very useful in the entrapment of Denbigh.

The duke was cantering along Rotten Row the following day. It was a beautiful morning and he appeared to have the park to himself. The air was warm and sweet and smelled of a mixture of soot and new leaves and grass. He glanced up at the clear blue sky, reflecting that one hardly ever saw a completely blue sky anywhere in England at any time of the year. A large parrot sailed slowly over his head. He reined in his mount and watched it. It was gray and red but had a ridiculous gold fringe of downy feathers on each leg. He could see it quite plainly now, for it circled round and round over his head, getting lower each time.

Someone has lost their pet bird, was his first thought; and then his next was, Perhaps that is Mrs. Manners's parrot.

The parrot stopped circling and began to fly off slowly in the direction of Park Lane. He set his horse in motion again and followed it. It sailed across a wide expanse of grass, then circled down again and landed on the shoulder of a female sitting on a bench.

The lady had her head bent and was wearing quite a modish bonnet. Mrs. Manners, he thought. He dismounted and started to lead his horse toward her. It struck him again that she must have been very fond of Manners to use his name instead of keeping her title. He did not know that Mr. Manners had insisted she do so, even after his death, that having been a provision in his will.

There was a large striped cat rolling in the grass in front of the bench, while a little French greyhound frolicked about. Tray and Peter of the letters, he thought.

The parrot flew off again, and she was bending down to pet the cat as he approached. He swept off his hat and bowed.

"Good morning!"

Verity looked up, and they both stared at each other in surprise. The duke was surprised to find not Charlotte, but a young lady with clever black eyes in quite a pretty face. Verity found herself looking at the gentleman from the posting house, the one she had dreamed about when she wrote to Denbigh.

"I thought you were Mrs. Manners," he said. "I am Denbigh, and you must be Miss Bascombe."

Verity shook his hand, all the time wondering at the strange coincidence that this handsome duke should be the man she had thought about so often.

"May I?" He gestured toward the place on the bench beside her.

"Certainly." Verity half rose, bobbed a token curtsy, and sat down again, her face a little flushed.

"Oh, don't do that," she cried, seeing the duke had lifted Peter onto his lap. "The cat will bite you."

The duke merely smiled at her lazily and stroked the cat, who half closed its eyes and began to purr.

He crossed his booted legs at the ankle, and the greyhound lay down and rested its chin on his boots and looked worshipfully up into his face.

"Goodness!" exclaimed Verity. "You do have a way with animals."

"I had not noticed it before. These seem particularly well behaved. I saw the parrot."

"Pretty Polly likes flying about," said Verity. "But it always returns."

"Is it male or female?"

"I confess I do not know. I forgot to ask the veterinarian. Polly is a name given to both sexes of parrot, I understand."

"Mrs. Manners is extremely fond of them."

"Yes," said Verity, for what else could she say?

"I am sorry I did not invite you to my party last night. But I was not aware of your existence until Mrs. Manners spoke of you."

"It does not matter," said Verity. She gave a charming laugh that lit up her expressive face and made her black eyes shine. "I believe I have been to enough parties, fetes, drums, routs, and ridottos to last me a lifetime."

"I am taking Mrs. Manners driving tomorrow. I would be honored if you would join us." Now why had he said that? he thought with irritation. Much better to have Charlotte to himself.

Then he realized the odd Miss Bascombe was surveying him with amusement. Verity was thinking how surprised the duke would be if he could guess how very angry Charlotte would become if Verity had dared to accept his invitation. "I have some

67

sewing to do, Your Grace. I am very honored by your invitation but must decline."

"Very well. As you will. Do you stay in London for very long, Miss Bascombe?"

"Not very long now," said Verity. "My father has gone to Scotland and our home is locked up. I wait daily for news of his return so that I may leave."

"Indeed! You seem almost anxious to shake the dust of London from your heels."

"It will be pleasant to be home again," said Verity wistfully. Now that she had met him, she yearned for home. She did not want to stay and watch him court Charlotte, although she would not admit this reason to herself.

"Have you been to Scotland yourself, Miss Bascombe?"

"No, Your Grace. I would be interested to visit the Highlands one day, to see, you know, if it is all as romantical as Mr. Scott would have us believe."

"I have been to the north, as far as Inverness. I think Dr. Johnson was nearer the mark than Mr. Scott."

Verity laughed. "I think the doctor's famous dislike of the Scotch was largely to tease his friend, Mr. Boswell, you know, when he said things like the noblest thing a Scotchman ever sees is the high road to England, or something like that."

"To return to your evident desire to go home," he said. "Does that mean you do not like London?"

"Oh, I like it immensely. There is so much to see. I went to the British Museum the other day. It was fascinating, although our German guide raced us past everything at a great rate, gabbling out descriptions in broken English. Why must they go on as if it is a race rather than a visit to a museum?"

"Because they collect tips from each party at the end of the tour. The more parties they race through

68

the building, the more money they have at the end of the day."

"How simple. I never thought of that."

They fell silent. It was an oddly companionable silence. The cat purred, the dog snored gently, and the parrot landed on the grass in front of them and regarded them with a quizzical eye.

At last, Verity stole a glance at his profile, noticing the proud nose, the square chin, and the firm mouth. His eyelashes, she saw, were almost as long and silky as Charlotte's. Most odd in a man. He had drawn off his gloves and the hand idly stroking the cat was white and strong.

"Where do you go this evening?" he asked, breaking the silence.

Verity gave a little sigh. "A ball. At the Whitakers'."

"I may see you there. Mr. Whitaker is a friend of mine. He wrote to me in the country asking me to attend, but, at that time, I had no intention of coming to London."

"And what changed your mind, about coming to London, I mean?" asked Verity, eager for praise of her powers as a correspondent.

He looked at her thoughtfully. "Mrs. Manners's charming descriptions of the capital changed my mind," he said.

"Yes, she *is* a very good letter writer, is she not?" asked Verity, greedy for more praise.

"Surprisingly so. They made me realize I had never known Mrs. Manners well at all."

Verity's elation at his praise for the letters disappeared, leaving her in a sudden black depression. She wanted to cry out, "*I* wrote them. Charlotte barely knows how to write!"

This is what comes of living in fantasy, thought Verity bitterly. Oh, if only my man from the posting house could be someone else. Aloud, she said quietly, "I must leave."

He put the cat on the grass, stood, and assisted her to her feet. Her hand trembled in his. "You are cold!" he exclaimed. "I have kept you here too long."

"No," said Verity. "I shall do very well. A brisk walk is all I need."

The great parrot hopped up onto her shoulder and nestled against her bonnet, making odd crooning sounds. Verity dropped an awkward curtsy, for it was hard to curtsy with the weight of the parrot throwing her off balance, and then walked away, with the little greyhound prancing at her heels and the cat slouching along behind.

He watched her go. She was small but had a very good figure, he thought idly. Her hair had been hidden by her bonnet and cap, for it was the fashion to cover the hair with a lace cap and then put a poke bonnet with a huge brim on top of it. He wondered what color it was. She moved with a fluid, sensual grace. When her cloak had fallen open as he talked to her, he hadn't been able to help noticing that her breasts were high and pointed.

He turned about to untether his horse. He saw the figure of Lady Wythe approaching and waited politely until she slowly came up to him. By the time she reached his side, Verity was a small figure in the distance, disappearing into the shadow of the lodge at Park Lane.

"I see I have missed Miss Bascombe," said the old countess crossly. "What a pity. I do enjoy our chats. Such a fine girl and so intelligent."

"Hardly a girl anymore, Countess."

"She is, I believe, twenty-four, still very young to one such as I. When I talk to her, I wonder if we have become worn-out and past our use. The aristocracy, I mean. Miss Bascombe is the daughter of a country lawyer. She has a tough, quick mind combined with warmth, courtesy, and kindness. She makes all the other young misses seem empty and vapid. A great pity I missed her."

The duke smiled. "I never thought to hear of you being so taken with anyone. You normally have an acid tongue."

The countess gave an infinitesimal shrug. "What did you make of the Manners female?"

"Very beautiful."

"And that is all you saw? Men!"

He was torn between irritation and amusement. "I shall no doubt learn more about Mrs. Manners when I see more of her."

"There isn't anything more to learn," said the countess. "What you saw last night was it."

"My dear Lady Wythe, when a lady is as beautiful as Mrs. Manners undoubtedly is, she seems to positively encourage uncharitable comments."

The countess sniffed. "Run along with you, do. You'll find out soon enough, Denbigh. You'll find out!"

Chapter Five

Verity did not have an opportunity to tell Charlotte of her meeting with the duke until they were seated together in the carriage taking them to the Whitakers' ball.

And now that she did have the opportunity, she found she was strangely reluctant to say anything. Verity was wearing the burgundy silk gown. She knew it became her better than anything she had ever worn before. She had made burgundy silk roses to ornament her hair. If she told Charlotte about the meeting, then Charlotte would ply her with questions and exclaim and criticize and might even send her home!

But when they left their wraps in a downstairs room in the Whitakers' mansion that had been assigned to the female guests and Verity saw the full glory of Charlotte's ensemble, she began to feel very silly. Who in their right mind was going to notice a provincial girl in a homemade gown when faced with such magnificence?

Charlotte was wearing a gown of silver spider gauze over a white slip. On her golden curls was a cunning headdress of silver gauze embroidered with silver thread and seed pearls. The gown was cut very low to show the whiteness of Charlotte's skin and the excellence of her bust.

Verity was only human. She had felt stabs of jealousy before, but never such a raging torrent as the bitter feeling of envy that now engulfed her. Jealousy was not a green-eyed monster, she thought. It was red in tooth and claw, with glaring, fiery eyes.

Her own gown seemed too demure and too modest in comparison. She tried to pull the neckline lower, but it would not move an inch.

Feeling dowdy and miserable, Verity trailed after Charlotte up the stairs to the ballroom. The duke would undoubtedly be there. He would dance with Charlotte. He would tell her of the meeting in the park. They would laugh together about this gauche companion who had not even mentioned the matter. Perhaps Charlotte would give that tinkling laugh of hers and tell Denbigh that her little companion was obviously smitten with him.

Verity went hot and cold by turns.

Mr. and Mrs. Whitaker were a young couple, good *ton*, but not very rich. They were very popular because they were scatterbrained and amusing. The ballroom was quite shadowy because the Whitakers had economized on candles. They had also economized by having country wildflowers to decorate the ballroom instead of expensive hothouse flowers. They had gone into the country themselves to pick them. But since neither could tell flower from weed, it was a very odd assortment that filled the vases and pots. They had also picked armfuls of bluebells, unaware that bluebells do not stay fresh for very long after they are picked, and so there were great vases of sadly wilting blooms standing in corners.

Mr. George Wilson was one of the first people Verity saw when she entered the ballroom. He *would* be here, she thought crossly. He would monopolize her. She would have no chance of dancing with the duke. And sure enough, Mr. Wilson came bounding over to secure two dances, one of them being the supper dance. He was so open and friendly that Verity began to feel ashamed of herself. How could she even begin to dream of competing with Charlotte? She decided she had been dazzled by the duke's title and because he had turned out to be that gentleman of the posting house she had woven so many fantasies around.

Verity decided that the best thing to do was to forget about the duke and Charlotte completely, be as pleasant and kind to Mr. Wilson as she could possibly be, and try to enjoy the dance. Verity knew she danced well. She tried not to let the fact that Charlotte danced even better enter her mind, but enter it it did. For Charlotte was having the honor of being the first lady the Duke of Denbigh asked to dance. It was a waltz. Verity wrenched her eyes from the beautiful spectacle they presented, shut her ears to the admiring comments about her, and finally succeeded in beginning to have a tolerably pleasant evening.

Verity's good intentions received a setback when the duke took Charlotte in to supper. She was seated well away from them, so she could only guess that they were getting along famously. She could not see the duke's expression, but she could see the radiant one on Charlotte's beautiful face.

The duke found himself being amazed at the gush of sheer trivia that was issuing from Charlotte's perfect pink lips. He did not have to say much, for Charlotte barely paused for breath. At last, when she had just finished a very long anecdote about going to a rout where the Prince Regent had looked at her *so*, he asked mildly, "I believe Miss Bascombe is present."

"Yes."

"She appears very fond of your pets."

"Miss Bascombe is dutiful and does her best to help me. As you will not be dancing with her, you will not meet her this evening. But you will be able to meet her tomorrow when you call to take me driving."

"And why will I not be dancing with her?" asked the duke, his mind registering surprise that for some reason Miss Bascombe had not told Mrs. Manners about their meeting in the park.

Charlotte giggled. "You forget. She is only a lawyer's daughter."

"But that does not give her two left feet or a squint." He was about to add that Miss Bascombe danced beautifully, but if he had guessed aright, he was not supposed to know what she looked like.

Charlotte was thinking rapidly that it was better one of the duke's dances should be taken up by Verity than by one of her rivals.

"Of course, Miss Bascombe would be thrilled if you danced with her. It would be something for her to remember for the rest of her life."

That artless remark almost made the duke decide *not* to ask Verity, but after supper he saw her sitting alone at the end of a row of chairs. A friend stopped him and by the time he had finished talking, the sets for the dance had been made up. The duke looked down at Verity and said ruefully, "I was on my way to ask you to dance but was waylaid, and now I am too late."

He sat down beside her. Her skin had a warm honey color and was flattered by the deep wine color of her gown. She sat as calmly and correctly as any young miss should, and yet there was a vitality and

75

a sensuality emanating from her that he found exciting.

"I gather you did not tell Mrs. Manners of our meeting in the park," he began.

"I didn't? It must have slipped my mind," said Verity in polite accents.

"Very unflattering," he replied with a laugh.

"Not really so unflattering. You see, I did not have an opportunity to say anything, but I suppose I had better now or it will appear strange."

"I should think it is of little consequence. I did not say anything about our meeting myself."

They smiled at each other like conspirators and then the duke felt a qualm of unease. He should not be siding with Miss Bascombe against Charlotte, even in such a trivial matter.

"You told me you had had an exhausting round of social events, Miss Bascombe," he went on. "You will, therefore, have seen little of London apart from the West End."

"Oh, no," said Verity. "I went to Euston one day to see Mr. Trevithick's engine, and then to the Tower, and I have been to St. Paul's churchyard to look at the secondhand bookstalls and . . ."

Her voice faltered and died away as she found him looking down at her quizzically.

"Ah, that is the reason Mrs. Manners went to all those unfashionable places she mentioned in her letters," he teased.

"Mrs. Manners was kind to go," said Verity miserably, feeling as if she were falling deeper into a black pit of lies. "But I would not say anything about it to her. It was not very fashionable of me to want to go to such places."

"Did you go to that dinner in honor of Monk Lewis?" he said.

"Yes, Your Grace."

76

"And how did you find our notorious author?"

"Very disappointing," said Verity. "I had expected a tall, brooding, gloomy creature instead of a funny little man with odd eyes."

"Like those of an insect?"

"Yes, that is exactly what I . . . er, what Mrs. Manners said." Verity sounded a trifle breathless.

"Mrs. Manners wrote enchanting letters to me," he said, watching her face. "When I read them, I felt I had never really known her. *That* was why I came to London, you know, to meet the authoress of those letters."

"And now you have," said Verity, a trifle crossly.

"Oh, yes, now I think I have."

"Charles!"

The duke looked up in irritation at a tall man who had approached them and then his face lit up. "James . . . James Castleton! How wonderful to see you. I thought you were at the wars."

"I was finally given some leave."

"Miss Bascombe, may I present my friend, Lord James Castleton. James, Miss Bascombe."

Verity held out her hand and Lord James dropped a light kiss on the back of her glove. He was tall and thin, with a rakish, mobile face and thick, springy black hair.

"Are you in London just for the Season, Miss Bascombe?" asked Lord James.

"I am not here precisely for the Season," said Verity carefully. "I am not coming out. My old friend, Mrs. Manners, was kind enough to invite me for a short stay."

"Oho!" said Lord James, cocking a quizzical eyebrow at the duke.

The duke looked annoyed, so Lord James added quickly, "We must meet tomorrow, Charles. In the afternoon, say?"

"No, alas, I am engaged to drive out with Mrs. Manners. But I have no plans for the evening."

The dance was over. Verity saw Mr. Wilson striding purposefully toward her. She rose and said, "I must join my partner. Good evening, Your Grace, my lord."

Both men watched her go. Verity was uncomfortably aware of this and behaved in a very warm and charming manner to Mr. Wilson.

"Attractive little thing," said Lord James, "but clever. Got clever eyes."

"Yes, she is very clever," said the duke, but he was startled that Lord James found Verity attractive and that her present partner appeared to be quite bewitched by her. He glanced around the ballroom as if hoping a glimpse of the dazzling Charlotte would overshadow Verity's strange appeal. Charlotte was tripping gaily through the steps of a country dance. She looked a picture of beauty. He found his eyes straying back to Verity.

Verity was glad to get to bed that night. "Charles," her mind kept repeating over and over again. "His name is Charles."

She heard a light step in the corridor. Charlotte!

Charlotte came in and walked forward and perched on the edge of the bed. "That was a successful evening," she said with a yawn. "So successful I forgot to tell you of *your* conquest, dear Verity."

"My conquest?"

"Mr. Wilson."

"Yes," said Verity, feeling depressed. "He is a very amiable man."

"Slyboots!" Charlotte giggled. "Mr. Wilson asked my permission to call on you tomorrow. I felt quite like a dowager. He is eminently suitable for you.

In fact, a step up in the world. The Suffolk Wilsons, you know."

"Do you mean Mr. Wilson is going to propose marriage?"

"What else? His mama is said to be a tartar, so be sure she does not ride to town as soon as the engagement is announced to horsewhip you."

"I don't want to marry Mr. Wilson," said Verity firmly.

"Good heavens, why not, you silly thing?"

"Mr. George Wilson," said Verity clearly, "is a worthy young man, pleasant, amiable, and dull. If I had wanted to marry a dull young man, I could have done so a long time ago. Furthermore, I am not in love with him."

"You should remember your position in life," said Charlotte sharply. "You cannot expect anything higher. This talk of love is ridiculous."

"But are you not in love with Denbigh?"

"Of course I am. I dote on the man. Fortunately, he is a wealthy duke, which is one of his greatest attractions. Do think seriously about Mr. Wilson, Verity dear, and remember that you cannot expect to do better."

She kissed Verity on the cheek and left the room.

After she had gone, Verity scrubbed her cheek angrily with her handkerchief. She began to feel remorseful about all the harsh things she had said about George Wilson. She dreaded the forthcoming proposal. Her other suitors in the past had not appeared to be in love with her. They had proposed, or so Verity believed, because she was of their social rank and endowed with a comfortable dowry. But Mr. Wilson had begun to show alarming signs of being in love—or of thinking he was in love.

Verity tried to sleep, but she tossed and turned for long stretches of the night, wondering how to turn down Mr. Wilson and yet leave that gentleman's pride intact.

Mr. Wilson was to call at two in the afternoon. Charlotte had quite made up her mind that Verity had come to her senses, for all Verity would say on the matter was that she wanted to see Mr. Wilson alone and did not need a chaperon. Charlotte expansively told her to use the Yellow Saloon and to entertain Mr. Wilson with any refreshments she cared to order.

Verity went downstairs to the kitchen and ordered a good bottle of wine to be decanted, biscuits, and fruit. "But do tell the servants to make sure Pretty Polly does not get any grapes," she added. "That bird is thoroughly spoiled and has been gorging itself on all the wrong things."

James, the second footman, was carrying a bowl of hothouse black grapes to the Yellow Saloon when the parrot sailed down, claws outstretched. "No, you don't!" cried James, darting into the saloon and slamming the door in the parrot's face.

Pretty Polly crouched behind a marble bust of Socrates in the hall and sulked. After a while, it dropped off to sleep. The opening of the street door awakened it.

Mr. Wilson was ushered in. Pretty Polly cocked its head to one side and watched as the double doors of the Yellow Saloon were thrown open.

"I shall tell Miss Bascombe you are here," Pomfret said.

Mr. Wilson strode up and down the Yellow Saloon, wondering whether to get down on one knee or not. He knew one thing: He would be heartily glad when the whole business was over. He thought of his mother's furious face and quailed.

He turned about to take another walk down the long room and saw the huge parrot, standing on the console table, greedily eating grapes. Mr. Wilson had affected to like the pets for Verity's sake. But privately he detested them. He was prepared to let her bring the dog and the cat to the marriage. The cat could go to the kitchens to keep down the mice, and the dog could go to the kennels where dogs belonged. But the parrot would have to go.

"Shoo!" he said, flapping his arms. Pretty Polly paid no attention. "Bloody parrot," said Mr. Wilson. "Just you wait!"

The great parrot raised its head and looked at him. "Pretty Polly," it squawked. And then came Verity's voice. "Mr. George Wilson is a worthy young man. Pleasant, amiable, and dull. If I had wanted to marry a dull young man, I could have done so a long time ago. Furthermore, I am not in love with him." The parrot gave a genteel cough and returned to the grapes.

The specter of an angry mother that had haunted Mr. Wilson's mind was suddenly replaced by a bright image of a loving and caring mother who hung on his every word and pandered to his every whim.

The parrot wrenched off a little bunch of grapes, hopped onto the floor, and walked under the sofa to enjoy the fruit in peace.

Verity came into the room, looking wan and tired. "Good day to you, Mr. Wilson. Please be seated."

"I cannot, ma'am," said Mr. Wilson. "I have merely called to tell you I am returning to the country to my dear mother."

Verity smiled her relief. "How very courteous of you."

"Yes, it is, isn't it?" said Mr. Wilson inanely. "Mrs. Manners seemed to have the ridiculous idea that I meant to propose to you. Can you think of anything more laughable?"

81

"Yes, I can, Mr. Wilson. Many things."

"But I said to myself, Miss Bascombe is a lady of good sense and well aware of her station in life. She would never be presumptuous enough to expect a proposal of marriage from one such as I."

"Do go away, Mr. Wilson," said Verity. "You are beginning to sound like a coxcomb."

"I shall go. Yes, I shall go," he said passionately. "My mother will find out how much her love and care of me is appreciated. Congratulations on your zoo," he sneered as he reached the door. "Most versatile. Ho! Most cunning."

He stomped off in a fury.

Verity slumped down in a chair, wondering whether to laugh or to cry.

There was no sign of the parrot.

Charlotte came dancing in wearing a large cap. She was enjoying her dowager act and had rehearsed a pretty speech to deliver to the happy pair. Her face fell when she saw Verity alone.

"What happened?"

"He was most rude," said Verity. "Quite passionately so. He said his intention in calling was simply to tell me that he was removing to the country. He said he was sure that I could not possibly be expecting a proposal of marriage because that would mean he was stooping too ridiculously low—not in those words, but I am too distressed to remember the exact ones."

"Vulgar little mushroom," said Charlotte venomously. "I never liked him, anyway. But don't you see, Verity, it has happened to *you*! I tell you, the next proposal I get will be in the middle of Hyde Park. Come now, you must admit it is very weird and scary. For Mr. Wilson was head over heels in love with you last night. Where is that parrot?"

"I do not know, Charlotte. What has Pretty Polly to do with it?"

"Perhaps the bird can talk and is creeping into the room and saying vile things about us."

Verity laughed. "What a vivid picture! It is just an ordinary, speechless parrot. It makes a few noises, but it never talks. And if it could talk, dear Verity, it would squawk stupid things in a parrot voice. I remember seeing a parrot at a fair. It said things like 'Pretty Polly,' and then it whistled awfully, and then said 'How de do' about a hundred times over. It's a parrot, not some sort of Iago."

"I suppose you are right. But what is happening in this house?"

"I agree that when you do receive another proposal, it should be somewhere outside," said Verity slowly. "But you know, we will probably find there is some person in society who has a spite against you and who gets wind of any proposal and visits the gentleman who is about to propose and tells him awful things about you. Because I am your friend, I received the same treatment."

"You have the right of it!" cried Charlotte. "This great beauty of mine is a curse. It creates such jealousy."

"Yes," said Verity dismally, thinking of her own outrageous feelings. But the episode of Mr. Wilson had brought her to her senses. She, Verity Bascombe, had been in danger of becoming quite spoony about the Duke of Denbigh. Verity felt free now.

"I think I shall take the pets out this afternoon for a long airing," she said.

"But you must be here when Denbigh calls," said Charlotte. "I promised him an introduction."

"Now don't tell me the great Duke of Denbigh is going to be upset because your companion is not around. I should think he would be delighted."

"But don't you see, it makes things more conventional if I am chaperoned," said Charlotte eagerly.

"I suppose so," said Verity, her heart sinking. "I will go early to the park and return in good time for his call."

Soon Verity was sitting on her favorite bench, telling Lady Wythe all about Mr. Wilson's odd visit and how she had come to the conclusion that some ill-wisher was telling spiteful tales about Charlotte and herself. James, the second footman, was not present, having been sent on an errand by Charlotte.

"Humph!" said the dowager. "There is a great deal of spiteful gossip about. But Mr. Wilson sounds to me like a man whose pride had been badly hurt. Are you sure you did not say something at the ball before the end that might have made him take you not only in dislike, but to wish revenge?"

Verity shook her head.

"Lady's maids can be treacherous creatures. Do you have one?"

"No. Mrs. Manners does, but her maid is an efficient, pleasant woman, well pleased with her post. Charlotte stole her away from young Lady Martin and is very proud of her prowess. The maid is also very clever and has told Mrs. Manners that the washes for the face she prepares contain a secret ingredient that will prolong the youth of the skin. It is in her interest to keep her mistress happy."

"All very odd. How goes Mrs. Manners's pursuit of Denbigh, and how did you fare with him yesterday in the park?"

"Denbigh calls today to take Mrs. Manners for a drive. I—I . . . did meet him here yesterday, but for some reason I neglected to tell Charlotte so."

"Well, that is because, for reasons best known to yourself, you wish to stay longer in London and you know that if Mrs. Manners suspected the slightest breath of intimacy between you and her duke, she would send you packing."

"The reason I am anxious to stay," said Verity crossly, "is quite simple. My father has not yet returned from Scotland."

"But you have friends and neighbors in that place . . . Market Basset?"

"Of course, but I could not leave the pets with Mrs. Manners or she would get rid of them, and I do not know of anyone who would house them."

"Mrs. Alder was at the Whitakers' ball last night and said that Denbigh spent quite some time talking to you."

"Not very long. His friend, Lord James, interrupted us."

"I wonder how long it will take him to find out that his dear correspondent is none other than yourself."

"Lady Wythe, let us talk of something other than Denbigh and Mrs. Manners."

"As you will. Rumor has it that Beau Brummell is in sore debt and being pressed by his creditors. He has ceased to be a clever gambler and become so vain, he tried to make the Prince Regent unfashionable. Now, of course, he has discovered that a malicious wit of no particular background can rise to eminence by hanging on to Prinny's coattails, but without the prince's favor, he begins to appear quite rude in an ordinary way."

"But why should that be!" exclaimed Verity. "The Prince Regent is generally reviled and lampooned almost daily in the press and in the print shops."

"But he *is* the Prince Regent, you see," said Lady Wythe, "and much as people sneer at royalty, they will fall over backward to seize a chance of getting close to court circles. Poor George. He has made a great many enemies."

They chatted amiably until a cloud covered the sun. Verity was reminded of the passing of time. She peered at the little fob watch pinned to her gown.

"I must go," she said, jumping to her feet, "or I will not have time to change!"

Lady Wythe smiled as she watched Verity crossing the park. The parrot landed on Verity's shoulder and the dog scampered at her heels. Verity turned around and looked back. She hesitated, walked on, and looked back again.

The cat! She is missing the cat, thought Lady Wythe.

Verity was wondering whether to go straight home and hope that Peter would find his own way back to Berkeley Square when Tray suddenly ran ahead to the line of trees in the park by Park Lane and began to circle one of the tallest sycamores, barking furiously.

Looking up, Verity saw the cat out on a branch. It was a dizzying distance above the ground. "Peter!" she called. "Come down, you silly animal." The cat let out a dismal howl that went straight to Verity's sentimental heart.

Lady Wythe came up accompanied by her elderly maid, Maria. Maria was usually sent off to take a walk when her mistress talked to Verity.

"You had better go home and send one of the footmen back to climb up to get the cat," said Lady Wythe. Peter howled again.

"Oh, please, Lady Wythe. Please ask your maid to hold the dog's leash while I climb up."

"Nonsense," said the dowager, much shocked. "Most unladylike."

"Please!"

"Oh, very well. But I shall go as far as Park Lane to see if I can find one of my friends. You need a groom or a footman to help you, or a chimney sweep's boy!"

Verity pushed Pretty Polly off her shoulder. Then she untied her bonnet and placed it carefully at the foot of the tree along with her cloak. She grasped one of the lower branches and swung herself up. Determined not to look down, she climbed higher and higher, glad of her slight figure and light weight as the branches became thinner. She finally reached the branch on which the cat was crouched. "Come along, Peter," she ordered. "There is nothing to fear."

The cat, its eyes dilated with terror, inched slowly toward her. Soon Verity was able to grasp the animal by the scruff of the neck and haul it onto her lap. "Now to get you down," she said, stroking the cat gently. "It cannot be so very far. I came up quite easily."

Verity looked down and then let out a shriek of terror. The cat, sensing her fright, shivered and dug its claws into her gown. The ground seemed miles below. Verity clutched the thin trunk with one hand and the cat with the other and closed her eyes.

Lady Wythe had stopped the Duke of Denbigh's carriage in Park Lane. She had many friends and there were several other carriages she could have stopped, but when her sharp eyes spotted the duke in the distance, she had decided that no one else would do.

The duke, on his way to keep his appointment with Charlotte, listened, amused, climbed down from his carriage, and walked into the park with Lady Wythe. He thought he would find Verity ineffectually trying to get as far as the lower branches.

"Dear goodness! There she is!" cried the old

countess, pointing aloft with her lavender silk parasol. The duke stared up at the tiny figure at the top of the tree. He shrugged off his coat, pulled off his Hessian boots, and began to climb.

Lady Wythe watched his ascent with great satisfaction. "Do but observe the muscles in his legs, Maria," she said to her maid. "Quite magnificent. Don't stand there with your mouth open. Give me my double glass. This deserves a better look."

Verity felt a shaking in the tree under her and opened her eyes and risked a look down. The Duke of Denbigh was climbing nimbly and quickly toward her, the sun glinting on his golden hair. She watched, forgetting her fear, as he climbed closer.

"Good day to you, Miss Bascombe," he said politely when he was directly beneath her. "Pass that creature down to me and I will take it to safety and return for you."

Verity lifted the cat by the scruff of its neck and handed it down to the duke. "I think, Your Grace," she said, "that if you climb down very slowly, I can find the courage to follow you."

He nodded and began to descend, holding the cat. Verity began to follow him. He wanted to look up to make sure she was safe, but did not dare. Very few ladies had adopted the modern fashion of wearing drawers and he did not want to embarrass Miss Bascombe. He finally swung nimbly down to the ground and put the cat on the grass. Verity had reached the lower branches. He held out his arms. "Jump, Miss Bascombe!"

Verity leaped down into his arms, and he held her very tightly against him. Soft breasts met hard chest; soft curls tickled his nose. Emotion, sweet, sharp, and intense, stabbed through his body. Then he felt her body shaking and set her a little away from him. "You are safe now," he said softly. "There is nothing to fear."

But Verity felt she had everything to fear. The violent, wanton yearning of her body startled and alarmed her. She put out a trembling hand to his shoulder and steadied herself for a moment. He covered her hand with his own, looking down at her with tenderness and a certain amount of surprise.

All very satisfactory, thought Lady Wythe. *Very!*

Chapter Six

Charlotte was in a fever of worry and impatience.
Four-thirty had come and gone. It was now a quar-
ter to five. Tears filled her large blue eyes and
poured down her cheeks. There was a curse on the
house. She would sell it.

A rumbling of carriage wheels sent her running
to the window again. There was the duke in a racing curricle with his liveried tiger at the back.
There beside him was a sooty and battered-looking
Verity with the parrot on her shoulder.

Charlotte ran out onto the front step. The duke
assisted Verity down from the carriage. Charlotte
noticed that he, too, had stains of soot on the cambric of his shirt, and bits of twigs were sticking onto
his coat.

"What happened, Your Grace?" she cried. "An
accident?"

"No, no, Charlotte," said Verity wretchedly. "It
was all my fault. Peter was stranded high in a tree
in the park. I went to rescue him and became stuck.
His Grace very kindly rescued me and the cat."

Charlotte closed her eyes. She wondered if it was
possible to die from sheer rage.

"Mrs. Manners," she heard the duke say, his voice warm with concern, "let me assist you into the house. Do not be so upset. Miss Bascombe is quite safe."

He put his hand under her elbow, and despite her bad temper, Charlotte was quick to use the opportunity to lean against him.

The duke was touched by Charlotte's evident distress, which he put down to worry over Miss Bascombe.

When they were all seated in the Yellow Saloon, the duke said, "As you can see from my dirt, I am not a fit escort for you, Mrs. Manners."

Charlotte rallied bravely. "Stay and take wine with me, Your Grace. We may have our drive on another day."

The greyhound walked past. Charlotte remembered she was supposed to dote on her pets. She held out her hand. The little greyhound shrank away, then ran to Verity and lay down at her feet.

The duke accepted a glass of wine from Pomfret. He could not help noticing that as the butler went to offer Verity a glass, Charlotte caught his eye and gave an infinitesimal shake of her head.

"Miss Bascombe was extremely brave," said the duke, deliberately tactless. "I can think of no other lady in London who would have attempted to climb that tree."

Charlotte shook an admonitory finger at Verity and said in silvery tones, "You are a sad romp. Only look at the ruin of your gown. Pray go immediately and lie down, Miss Bascombe."

Verity stood, and the duke rose as well. She curtsied and said in a low voice, "I am deeply indebted to you, Your Grace."

"It was an honor to be of service to you, Miss Bascombe."

Verity left the room. The duke noticed that the parrot, dog, and cat went with her.

"Your pets seem much attached to Miss Bascombe," he said when the door had closed behind Verity.

"Yes," said Charlotte. "Poor Miss Bascombe is so awkward and ill at ease with humans that it is as well she has a talent for engaging the affection of dumb animals."

The duke thought quickly. What a spiteful remark! If he sprang to Verity's defense, then Charlotte would send her packing. He wanted to see Miss Bascombe again. So he smiled at Charlotte and said, "Miss Bascombe is an engaging and clever lady. Her affection for you needs no explanation. Lord James was saying to me only the other night that Mrs. Manners must be an exceptional lady to have such a clever and devoted companion. It is always easy to command the loyalty of the stupid."

"Dear Verity." Charlotte sighed. "I do not know what she would do without me."

Now my correspondent would never have said anything so vain, thought the duke. But aloud he said, "The weather has changed for the better. Perhaps I may be allowed to make up for today by driving you to Richmond Park on the morrow?"

Charlotte's eyes glittered with triumph. A long drive on a sunny day alone with the Duke of Denbigh! Great things could come of it.

"I had another engagement," she said cautiously, "but I could easily cancel it."

"I would not dream of upsetting your arrangements," he cried.

"It is nothing," said Charlotte quickly. "At what time may I expect you?"

"At ten in the morning."

Charlotte blinked. Ten in the morning seemed like the crack of dawn to her.

"Very well, Your Grace," she said with a smile. "Let us hope the weather remains fine."

Upstairs in her room, Verity looked gloomily at the pets. "If you knew what was good for you," she told them sadly, "you would not stay in here. The storm is about to break."

For Verity was sure the minute the duke left, an enraged Charlotte would come rushing in.

But although she heard the duke leave and waited a long time after that, there was no sign of Charlotte. At last, Charlotte's maid entered with a message from her mistress that Miss Bascombe was to get ready to go out to the opera at eight o'clock.

Feeling puzzled but relieved, Verity sat down at the dressing table and began to brush her hair. But the next feeling was one of sharp hope. Would the duke be there?

But the duke was not at the opera that evening. As Charlotte and Verity were entering the theater, the duke was sitting opposite his friend, Lord James, in Watier's. "Let me see if I have heard you aright," Lord James was saying. "You want me to go to Richmond with you tomorrow. I am to pretend to be enamored of Miss Bascombe, but once we are on the outing, I must appear to switch my affections to Mrs. Manners."

"A small thing to ask," said the duke equably. "Have some more of this excellent port."

"May one ask why?"

"One may. The reason I returned to London was that Mrs. Manners sent me delightful and interesting letters. As you know, I once proposed marriage to her and was turned down. I had since come to think of her as greedy and empty-headed and congratulated myself on my escape. But the letters led

93

me to believe I had been mistaken in her. She *is*, you must admit, very beautiful."

"Very."

"And so I returned to London. At first I thought Mrs. Manners was suffering from nerves and that was why she only spoke trivia. But when I spoke to Miss Bascombe, it dawned on me that it was more than likely Mrs. Manners had invited her old school friend to London in order to use her as a correspondent."

"But why?"

"Because Mrs. Manners now wants my title and fortune. It is no little thing to be a duchess."

Lord James frowned. "If, as you say, Miss Bascombe wrote those letters, then it does not say very much for Miss Bascombe's character to be party to such a plot, such a deception."

"I had not thought of that."

"Well, I would think of it now. Miss Bascombe obviously considers your title and fortune fair game to be secured for her friend by any methods possible."

"Put that way, it sounds quite dreadful."

"I can understand your interest in Mrs. Manners. She is the most exquisite thing I have ever seen. But the clever and plotting Miss Bascombe! That is another thing. Perhaps it was she who suggested the whole thing to Mrs. Manners in order to come to London for the Season. One could hardly call her good *ton*. Someone told me she is nothing but a country lawyer's daughter."

"She has warmth and spirit. I rescued her today from the top of a tree in Hyde Park."

"What was she doing up a tree?"

"Attempting to rescue Mrs. Manners's cat. She climbed so high she lost her nerve. Old Lady Wythe waylaid me in Park Lane and told me of Miss Bascombe's predicament, so I climbed up and brought the cat down, which gave Miss Bascombe enough courage to follow me."

"Most unbecoming in her," drawled Lord James. "And very hoydenish. Perhaps it was staged so as to force you to rescue her."

"Now you are being ridiculous."

"Lady Wythe knows everyone in London. How odd she should come out onto Park Lane for help at the precise moment you happened to be passing."

"She didn't, actually. I saw her standing at the edge of the road from quite a distance away."

"And who was before you in the carriages?"

"There was—let me see—Byng, Brown, Petersham, and Downie."

"And is there one of these gentlemen the old dowager does *not* know?"

"Well . . . no."

"Then there you are! I agree that Miss Bascombe, since she seems to have become your interest, has a certain attraction. It is all very well for a man to be clever, but it is a disaster in a woman. You would not want a wife with an independent mind!"

"I think it might be very interesting, and life would hardly ever be dull."

"Aha, but a plotting and scheming wife?"

"I still would like to go on this outing tomorrow and find an opportunity to tax Miss Bascombe with the fact that I believe her to have written the letters and listen to her explanation. Of course, if you have other plans . . . ?"

"No, I am intrigued by the plot. And if Miss Bascombe is as cunning as I am beginning to think she is, then you will need my protection."

"Good." The duke signaled to a waiter and ordered paper and pen. "I will let Mrs. Manners know of the new arrangements."

"You have been very quiet all evening, Charlotte," said Verity, as they returned home from the opera. "Yes this, no that. But a definite frost in the air. I did say I was sorry that I spoiled your drive, but just think: If I had not done so, then Denbigh might not have offered to drive you to Richmond, a much more satisfactory arrangement."

"You keep making me look like a fool," Charlotte burst out. "Those pets! You deliberately set out to steal their affection away from me."

"Fustian. You know very well that when I arrived, they were mangy and likely to die. In fact, you ordered them killed!"

"I never said such a thing. You are a liar. There! It is high time someone told you how lying and devious you are, Verity."

"Do not accuse me of your own character defects. You are cruel and selfish and ungracious, and I shall leave tomorrow," said Verity, tears glistening in her eyes.

"Good riddance," said Charlotte. "What is it, Pomfret?"

"This note from the Duke of Denbigh was delivered by hand, ma'am."

"Then why didn't you say so, you lummox, instead of creeping about furtively?"

"What does it say?" asked Verity.

"Mind your own business, miss."

"I hope he is writing to say he has changed his mind," said Verity.

Charlotte's eyebrows almost vanished up under her turban as she read.

"Goodness gracious. He is bringing Lord James

Castleton with him, for Lord James wishes to further his acquaintance with you. *You*, of all people!"

"Then," said Verity in a choked voice, "you may tell His Grace I was so tired of your bad manners that I left."

Charlotte looked at her in amazement. "Don't you want to go to Richmond with a handsome lord?"

"Not with you," said Verity, her hands clenched into fists.

"Oh, my dear Verity, you must not pay attention to my rubbish. I am jealous of you. There! I see I have amazed you. Odd, is it not? Like Beauty being jealous of the Beast. No! No! I was only funning. Come into the drawing room, I have something most important to tell you."

Pride was telling Verity that she should go up to her room and pack. But pride would not help her to see the duke again.

She followed Charlotte into the drawing room. Charlotte drew Verity down onto a backless sofa and held both her hands and gazed into her eyes. "Listen, my friend," she said. "I am head over heels in love with Denbigh. *That* is why I behaved so irrationally! Can you understand?"

Oh, yes, Verity thought sadly. *That* she could very well understand. "I will need your help on the morrow," said Charlotte urgently.

Verity looked at her miserably. She had not thought Charlotte capable of love, but how could any woman help loving the Duke of Denbigh? She did not know that Charlotte was only in love with the duke's title. Charlotte thought only very common people fell in love and so had claimed to be in love with the duke to give Verity's inferior middle-class mind something she could comprehend.

Then Verity realized that if she stayed in London, she would have a front-row seat at the courtship of the duke and Charlotte. Unbearable.

"No, Charlotte," she said. "I wish you well. But I must leave."

"Oh, my wicked tongue. My darling Verity. You know I do not have much time for my own sex. But I am very fond of you. We have had such fun, have we not? Do not be too rash. Stay at least for tomorrow. You know you admired my pink silk parasol. It is yours. There! See how I dote on you? Oh, Verity, do not be so cruel."

Charlotte raised a wisp of cambric to her eyes and began to sob.

Verity herself cried with great pain and difficulty. She did not know that Charlotte could cry at will. Her heart was softened. Charlotte should have the duke. Jealousy has made me as bad as Charlotte, thought Verity penitently. "Please do not cry, Charlotte. I will stay. Only do stop crying."

So Charlotte stopped. Her tears switched off as if she had turned off a tap in her head.

"We shall celebrate the renewal of our friendship."

Pomfret came in at that moment, followed by two footmen carrying the tea tray. But Charlotte waved them away and ordered champagne and two tankards.

"I shall be quite drunk," said Verity, raising a brimming silver tankard.

Charlotte giggled. "I adore champagne. Let us see who can drain the tankard dry first."

Verity laughed and spluttered as the bubbles went up her nose. Charlotte refilled their tankards. "To us!" she said.

Verity giggled, already feeling tipsy and lightheaded. "To us," she echoed.

"And you must give me your solemn pledge that

you will do everything in your power to help me ensnare the duke."

"You are really in love with him?"

Charlotte crossed her heart.

"Then I shall!" cried Verity, feeling noble.

Charlotte rang for more champagne. They were both very drunk by the time they reeled upstairs, giggling and laughing and still swearing eternal friendship.

In the privacy of her bedroom, Charlotte lay in bed and laughed and laughed. "The silly ninny," she said, meaning Verity. "I did very well. That should put paid to any ambitious ideas that creature might be harboring in her common mind! I really do believe silly Verity had some idea of getting Denbigh for herself!"

It was a perfect morning when two very fragile ladies emerged into the bright sunlight of Berkeley Square. Verity felt wretched. The light hurt her eyes and her mouth was dry.

Charlotte had a pounding headache. Both ladies hung on to the side of the carriage as it moved off. The duke's coachman was driving the open carriage. Both men were sitting with their backs to the horses and Verity and Charlotte facing them.

Despite her headache, Charlotte looked very beautiful. She was wearing her favorite sky-blue color: sky-blue gown, sky-blue gloves and shoes, and sky-blue parasol. Verity was dressed in a pink muslin gown and pelisse. The color did not flatter her, and her eyes were almost as pink as her dress.

The duke found her dull and quite unattractive. Charlotte sparkled in comparison. The attention of two handsome men was just the tonic she needed. As Verity began to feel sick with the motion of the carriage, Charlotte was quite restored to her usual good health.

At last the duke noticed that Miss Bascombe had turned a greenish color. He suggested they stop at an inn for some refreshments. Verity nodded gratefully.

As the duke was helping Verity down from the carriage, he took the opportunity to say, "You do not look very well, Miss Bascombe."

"I feel dreadful," said Verity candidly. "I drank too much champagne too late last night."

"Wicked Miss Bascombe, to succumb so easily to the fleshpots of London. I had thought you made of sterner stuff."

"Well, Your Grace, as you can see I am not, and feel likely to die."

"We shall have hock and seltzer and you will soon be recovered."

"What are you talking about?" cried Charlotte.

"Restoratives," said the duke. "I am recommending hock and seltzer."

The drink worked like a charm. Verity felt a warm glow taking the queasiness out of her stomach. The duke was amused by the transformation. Miss Bascombe's skin glowed with health once more, and her black eyes sparkled. Lord James caught a warning look from the duke and correctly interpreted it as a reminder that he was to appear interested in Verity at this stage of the outing. He reluctantly wrenched his eyes away from Charlotte's beautiful face and said, "I feel sure you are a lady of many secrets, Miss Bascombe. You are not perhaps one of those wicked novelists?"

"Not I," said Verity.

"But you like to write?"

"Not at all," said Verity uncomfortably. "I am supposed to be keeping a diary of all I see in London to read to my friends at our sewing circle back at Market Basset, but I regret to say I have not even begun."

"And have you had many fascinating experiences?"

"Oh, yes," said Verity. "London is full of things to see and do."

"And is there anything you have not seen which you would like to visit?"

"Yes, I would like to see the mint. They have just moved the mint, you know, from the Tower to Tower Hill. There are presses designed by the engineers Boulton, Watt, and Rennie, which, I believe, are steam-driven and able to strike coins at the staggering rate of a hundred a minute!"

Lord James looked amused. "But what of Almack's? The opera? The opening dinner at the Royal Academy?"

"Most enjoyable," said Verity. "But new inventions are intriguing, are they not?"

"Hardly a feminine interest."

"Being a female does not mean that one is mentally defective, Lord James."

He colored angrily, then remembered he was supposed to flirt with her and said, "I find beauty such as yours allied to brains somewhat intimidating, Miss Bascombe."

"I am not clever at all," said Verity in surprise, "and my looks are nothing out of the common way."

Lord James looked crossly at the duke, who was murmuring things to Charlotte on the other side of the table. It was too much to ask of him! Dalliance with Miss Bascombe was about as easy as wading through a sea of mud.

"You must trust me to be your looking glass, Miss Bascombe."

"Very prettily said, my lord," said Verity, "but I

am afraid my opinion of my looks is still the same, much as I long to believe you."

"Beauty is in the eye of the beholder," he said sententiously, casting a longing look in Charlotte's direction.

"Perhaps," said Verity. "But it must be very pleasant to be as beautiful as Mrs. Manners because then one can take all compliments at face value."

He brightened visibly. "Mrs Manners is divinely fair. Have you known her long?"

"We attended the same seminary in Bath," said Verity. "This visit is the first opportunity I have had of seeing her since I was there."

"And has she changed?"

"As to character, no," said Verity. "But her beauty is much greater."

He smiled at her warmly, thinking that Miss Bascombe certainly made up in loyalty and friendship what she lacked in charm.

As they returned to the carriage, Verity was irritated with herself. Lord James was supposed to have come on this outing to further his acquaintance with her. She, Verity, had received many fulsome compliments from some of her admirers in Market Basset. She had responded to them in the correct flirtatious manner. But love had never spoiled any of her conversation with gentlemen before and she had to admit to herself ruefully that she was wishing both Lord James and Charlotte at the devil. She reminded herself sternly that she had promised to support Charlotte in every way, and languishing after a handsome duke who was well above her touch was hardly the right way to go about it.

Verity had to confess that the duke seemed to be enjoying Charlotte's light prattle and was answering in kind as they bowled along the sunny road to Richmond. Lord James's behavior was beginning to puzzle Verity more and more. He paid her compliment after compliment, but his eyes kept straying to Charlotte when he was not trying to catch the duke's eye, almost as if he were begging permission to do something.

Lord James was waiting eagerly for the moment when he was supposed to switch his attention from Charlotte to Verity. As they strolled under the trees through Richmond Park, he thought it would never come. The duke and Charlotte were walking ahead, laughing and joking. Verity had taken herself firmly in hand and was behaving toward Lord James just as a young miss ought. She talked of balls and parties and people in society. But he answered her in an abstracted sort of way, then seemed to remind himself of something and paid her another compliment, stunning in its praise but insulting in the halfhearted, abstracted way in which it was delivered.

They returned to the carriage and went on to an inn situated at the edge of the Thames. The duke called for iced champagne, as the inn boasted its own icehouse. Verity drank sparingly, but Charlotte drank a great deal, her eyes glowing.

Then Lord James saw the message in the duke's eyes and heaved a sigh of relief. He jumped to his feet. "Charles has had too much of your attention, Mrs. Manners," he cried. "Pray walk with me a little and we will look at the swans."

Charlotte, elated at having two titled men competing for her favors, thought it would do the duke no harm to have a little competition and graciously agreed.

Verity and the duke were left alone together.

"My friend seems much taken with you," said the duke.

"I do not think so," said Verity, "although he is going to great lengths to make that appear to be the case. I wonder why?"

"Miss Bascombe! You cannot rate your attractions so low."

"When Mrs. Manners is about, I can and do."

"What an awkward sort of female you are, climbing trees, bristling up at compliments, and writing other people's letters for them."

Verity choked on her champagne. He waited politely until she had recovered and said, "You must think me a great fool if you believe that I thought those letters came from Mrs. Manners. She could not possibly have written them, but you most certainly could."

"You must not tease Mrs. Manners with this," said Verity.

"I would not dream of it. But to tease you, Miss Bascombe, gives me a great deal of pleasure."

They fell silent. The water chuckled past and the sun sparkled on the little waves.

They were sitting in the inn garden under an ash tree. The shadows of the leaves fluttered across Verity's face.

"Well," she said reluctantly, "Mrs. Manners has difficulty in writing letters. Quite a lot of people do, you know. So, yes, I wrote them, but they were really from her."

"And did you not stop to think such behavior deceitful?"

"No. Had Mrs. Manners not been interested in communicating with you, yet I had gone ahead and written the letters just the same—that would have been deceitful."

"But I was cleverly wooed in print and came hot-foot to London to meet my charming correspondent."

"I did not mean to do wrong," said Verity. "You loved her once."

"I thought I did, yes. Had Mrs. Manners written herself, then I am sure her letters would have betrayed that she was simply interested in becoming my duchess."

"You are too hard."

"Not I! She would not have even troubled to commiserate with me over my recent bereavement. You did. Who did you lose?"

"My mother."

"I thought the writer spoke from experience, but I was led to believe that Mrs. Manners had been shaken by the loss of her husband."

"Oh, I *am* sorry," said Verity. "Can we not forget those wretched letters?"

"We can try," he said with a charming smile. "What do you want to talk about?"

"I want to know why you instructed Lord James to pay court to me and then gave him permission to give up and go after Mrs. Manners."

His eyes glinted with amusement as he looked at her. "I think I shall tell the truth. I wanted some time alone with Mrs. Manners so that I could make up my mind once and for all about the author of those letters. Then I wanted some time alone with you. As you see, it has worked to a nicety. Lord James is enjoying the company of Mrs. Manners and I have found my letter writer."

"I thought we were not going to talk about those letters."

"Ah, but I had to in order to give you a truthful explanation. Do you hope to marry, Miss Bascombe?"

"You are blunt. There is no other career open to a gently bred female."

"And yet you have not really answered my question. The truth, Miss Bascombe!"

The truth was that if she could not marry him, then she really did not think she wanted to marry anyone.

"I am comfortably situated at home, Your Grace, and am fortunate in that I have no need to marry. Papa is trying to force my hand by saying that he means to marry again himself. That is because he fears for me. He thinks any woman who does not marry and have children is doomed to unhappiness."

"But you do not?"

"I think to be married to someone one does not really care for might be a very great unhappiness. Better to remain single."

"Yes," he said thoughtfully. "I think we are both very fortunate. Here comes our happy couple. Do you attend the Cunninghams' affair tonight?"

"I do not know, Your Grace. Mrs. Manners says where we are to go."

"Then I shall ask her. There is to be dancing, you know, and I have not yet had the pleasure of a dance with you."

Charlotte and Lord James came up to them, obviously well pleased with each other's company. Verity's heart gave a little surge of hope. She would rather the duke remained unmarried than watch him propose to Charlotte.

But on the road back to London, the duke once more devoted himself to Charlotte, teasing her and making her laugh. Lord James sat moodily with his arms crossed, staring out at the passing countryside. From time to time, Verity addressed some remark to him, but he answered her in an abstracted way.

She was glad when the carriage once more swung into Berkeley Square. The day was still sunny and warm, and Gunter's, the confectioner at number seven, was doing a brisk trade in ices.

Before the gentlemen left, Charlotte said they would be at the Cunninghams' that evening.

"Very successful, indeed." Charlotte sighed happily as she made her way upstairs. "A duke and a lord and both for the asking. But a duchess is such a good title, don't you think, Verity? Verity!"

But Verity had gone ahead to her room, and the slamming of her door was Charlotte's only reply.

Chapter Seven

Sir Richard Cunningham was a member of Parliament. Verity hoped that this introduction to political circles would provide her with enough interest to take her mind off the Duke of Denbigh.

But it turned out to be very much like any other London ball held during the Season. Ballroom draped in rose silk, banks of hothouse flowers against the walls, music by Neil Gow and his fiddlers, and catering by Gunter. The ladies simpered and the gentlemen stared. The Cunninghams were parvenus, and a line of improbable-looking ancestors looked down from the walls. Sir Richard had bought portraits of everyone else's ancestors to claim as his own. There was even a Haitian prince, his brown skin gleaming against a pink silk and gold-embroidered coat of the last century. Harriet wondered how the Cunninghams described him and how they had come by the portrait. Had there been a sale at some embassy? And would the Haitians not have had something to say about a member of their royal household decorating the walls of an M.P.'s home? Verity recognized the prince, having seen a steel engraving of him in a library book describing his visit to London some forty years before.

She saw Lady Wythe sitting with the dowagers and went to join her. "Why do the Cunninghams have a Haitian prince among their supposed ancestors?" asked Verity.

"Now how do you know they are not really the Cunningham ancestors?" asked the old dowager, looking amused.

"Mrs. Manners told me that their hunt round the salesrooms for ancestors is well known."

"Yes, for once her gossip is correct. I myself asked them about the prince. Sir Richard became very fidgety and claimed the prince was an American Indian who had once saved his life. Such a liar! No wonder he is in the House of Commons. He gets along famously with all the other liars, hence his popularity."

"But people in society will cut their own relatives in the street for being too unfashionable. What, then, is the charm of the Cunninghams?"

"Money. Sir Richard has a great many woolen manufactories in the north. He bought his title and favor at court. He lives here in Grosvenor Square and entertains lavishly. He is so vulgar and pushing that everyone feels comfortable about despising him while accepting his hospitality. He makes even the minor gentry feel superior, hence his success. I have noticed, Miss Bascombe, that from the first time I met you, you appear to take these grand affairs in your stride. I would have thought you would have found them quite intimidating after Market Basset."

"I have been to the assemblies in Bath," said Verity abstractedly, her eyes searching the room. "It is much the same thing."

"If you are looking for Denbigh," said Lady

Wythe, "then you are searching in the wrong direction. He is over there on your right."

Verity's head turned to the right as if being jerked round on wires. The duke was wearing a black evening coat. His cravat was beautifully tied, and a diamond pin blazed from among its snowy folds. His knee breeches and white silk stockings showed the strength of his thighs and the muscles in his legs. His golden hair was pomaded and gleamed in the light shed by hundreds of candles. "What a truly magnificent creature," murmured the countess.

Verity looked from the duke around the rest of the room at the haughty, beautiful, elegant ladies. Charlotte was over in a corner, talking to a group of men. Her hair, as golden as the duke's, was artlessly dressed in a disarray of artistic curls and topped with a little tiara of diamonds. Around her white neck shone a diamond necklace. Her gown was of simple white muslin worn over a rose-colored silk underdress.

Verity was wearing a gown of old-gold silk. In the privacy of her room, she had felt she looked very fine, but now she felt sadly diminished by the fresh pretty whites and pastel muslins all about her.

The duke set out toward Charlotte, but Lord James was there before him, soliciting Charlotte to dance. He turned about, his eyes raking the room and then falling on Verity.

"He is going to ask you to dance," said Lady Wythe.

"Yes," said Verity. "Since he could not reach the mistress in time, he comes in search of the companion."

"Do not be silly. Denbigh is not the slightest bit interested in Mrs. Manners and your common sense should tell you so."

110

Verity's intellect certainly told her so, but her jealous emotions told her at the same time that no man in his right mind would look at *her* with such a beauty as Charlotte Manners around.

And then before the duke could reach Verity, a young man appeared in front of her asking her to dance. There was nothing Verity could do but accept. Had she refused him, then the social laws would have forced her to refuse to stand up with any other man who asked her.

It was a country dance that lasted about half an hour. It was followed by another country dance, and, to Verity's extreme frustration, she found her hand claimed for that one as soon as the first was over. Good manners helped her to behave prettily to her partners. Verity had rapidly become a well-known figure in society because of her outings to Hyde Park with the strange assortment of pets. She had gradually become popular with the gentlemen without quite being aware of the fact.

Lady Wythe took great satisfaction in watching Verity's success. But Verity was not enjoying herself. She had promised herself one dance with the duke before putting him from her thoughts.

She was taken in to supper by an ebullient colonel who talked military matters during the whole meal and who, despite her silence, seemed greatly taken with her.

The first dance after supper was to be a waltz. Verity longed to waltz with the duke, to feel his arm at her waist, to have that memory to take back with her to Market Basset to warm the long, spinster years ahead.

People were beginning to rise from the supper tables to go back to the ballroom. The colonel talked on. The duke disappeared, then Charlotte, then Lord James, and still the colonel talked. At last, he looked around in amazement at the nearly empty room and said, "By George, Miss Bascombe, my next partner will be looking for me."

As Verity entered the ballroom, the duke was circling the floor with Charlotte in his arms. Her radiant face was turned up to his. His arm was at *her* waist.

Verity could not bring herself to dance with anyone else. She quietly moved away to the end of the long room, behind the banks of flowers, to where long curtains hung at the windows.

She slipped behind the curtains and found herself in an embrasure. Through the glass, she could make out the black shapes of sooty trees in the garden. She stood there for a long time, not wanting to go back to the ballroom until the waltz was finished.

Verity did not notice that the trees were bending down to the ground under a fierce wind. The air of the ballroom felt hot and suffocating. She wanted a breath of fresh air. The long windows opened outward like doors. She pushed one wide open and then gasped in alarm. A tearing gale swept past her, sending the curtains billowing out. She tried to close the window, but the force of the gale screaming past her made it impossible. Behind her in the ballroom were shrieks of dismay as all of the candles were blown out and the room was plunged into darkness.

And then a hand pulled her back and the duke's voice said, "Allow me, Miss Bascombe."

He wrenched the window shut and then called into the ballroom, "The window is closed. You may light the candles again."

Then he let the curtain fall and faced Verity, his face a white blur somewhere above her own.

"I did not know it was so very windy," said Verity. "I am sorry."

He found he still had a hand on her shoulder, but he did not take it away.

"I did want that dance with you, Miss Bascombe, but I could not get near you."

"It does not matter," said Verity, wishing he would take his hand away from her bare shoulder, for his touch was making her tremble.

"It matters very much to me," he said softly. He bent quickly and kissed her on the mouth.

It was only a brief kiss, but it rocked Verity to the soles of her feet. Shock was quickly followed by a wave of searing sweet passion mixed with yearning.

"How disgraceful we are," he said lightly. "Come, Miss Bascombe. I shall call on you tomorrow." He pulled aside the curtain. The ballroom was already half lit. Footmen with long tapers were scurrying back and forth, lighting the candles. The end of the ballroom where they stood was still shadowy enough to allow them to walk through the curtains into the ballroom again without everyone noticing.

Charlotte, however, saw them. She saw the dazed look on Verity's face and the tender one on the duke's. The fact that Denbigh might propose to the undistinguished Verity struck her like a hammer blow. How society would laugh at her! A middle-class nobody snatching such a prize from under her very nose.

Her first thought was to turn Verity out of the house that very night. But people might learn of it, the duke might learn of it, and that would not help matters. Charlotte continued to dance and to flirt while her mind worked busily.

The gale had blown itself out by the time they made their way the short distance to Berkeley Square. Verity longed to bury her head under the blankets and sleep and sleep. But Charlotte wound

113

an affectionate arm about her waist as soon as they were indoors. "We shall have tea, my friend," she said, "and you shall tell me all about your success."

"*My* success. It was as nothing compared to yours, Charlotte."

"Fiddle," said Charlotte over her shoulder as she led the way into the drawing room. "My only success was my waltz with Denbigh. How close he held me! Quite shocking of him. Oh, I am so in love with him, Verity, it would break my heart were anything to happen to ruin my chances."

"Are you really?" asked Verity sadly. "Are you really in love with him?"

Charlotte leaned forward and gazed into Verity's eyes. "Oh, I am so very much in love with him. I dream about him constantly. My blood is in a fever. I say his name over and over again to myself. But you cannot know what I mean."

Verity felt Charlotte spoke the truth. She spoke of feelings that only a woman deeply in love could experience. If Verity had gone into Charlotte's bedroom and had read the romance on the bedside table, she would have read exactly the same words on page 102. But since Charlotte was describing Verity's own feelings, she found it all too easy to believe her.

"When I am married," Charlotte went on, "you must come and live with us."

"Why, Charlotte? You will have a husband and a family."

"Because, Verity, I love you with all my heart. You are a good and loyal friend, and I know you would never do anything to cause me a moment's distress. When you swore to help me in my pursuit of Denbigh, I felt comforted and sustained. Sometimes I feel so alone in the world." Charlotte's eyes glistened with tears as she threw her arms around Verity. "My dear friend, my *very* dear friend."

Verity patted her awkwardly on the shoulder. She desperately wanted to escape, but Pomfret came in with the tea tray.

Over tea, Charlotte continued to smile caressingly at Verity and to praise her. A gray dawn was rising over London by the time Verity was at last able to escape to bed. She could feel the duke's lips against her own. He had said he would call, but he could not mean marriage. Dukes did not marry the Verity Bascombes of this world.

Charlotte picked up the novel from her bedside table and flicked through the pages, looking for more dialogue that might prove useful. A shadowy movement in the corner of the room caught her eye. She raised the candle and saw that it was the parrot.

She threw the book at it, and it squawked and flew up on top of the wardrobe. Charlotte looked around for other things to throw but realized just in time that if the bird squawked again, Verity might come running and Charlotte had had enough of Verity for one night.

She climbed out of bed and opened the door to let the bird out. As she lay in bed again, she found it was still sitting on the wardrobe, regarding her curiously.

"Why don't you flap along to dear Verity?" sneered Charlotte. She clasped her hands behind her head and said, "I wish I had never invited Verity. I can't stand her with her oh-so-good ways. She's been making sheep's eyes at Denbigh. He *can't* be interested in her. She's such a drab little frump. I mean, compared to me, she's nothing. I never liked her, anyway—Miss Prunes and Prisms.

She only pretends to be intelligent, but she's stupid really. And common! Only a country lawyer's daughter. I feel soiled by having her around. I shall continue all this 'dear Verity' friendship act until I can gracefully send her packing. I think I did well. She swallowed every word. As if one such as I could ever love one such as she! But at least I have made sure she will no longer encourage Denbigh."

A shadow crossed Charlotte's face as the parrot flew out of the room.

The Duke of Denbigh presented himself in Berkeley Square at eleven o'clock the following morning. He had a shrewd idea that Charlotte would still be asleep at that time but hoped that Verity kept country hours.

Pomfret took his card and ushered him into the Yellow Saloon.

As the butler opened the double doors, the parrot flew over his head and perched on the back of a chair.

Pomfret eyed Pretty Polly doubtfully. "I can try to get rid of that bird, Your Grace."

"Leave it," said the duke. "I have a feeling the sooner I get used to having it around, the better."

When the butler had left, the duke took a piece of tissue paper out of his pocket and unwrapped a date, which he held out to the parrot. "I know she will want to take you with her," he said, "so we may as well be friends."

Pretty Polly ate the date greedily, then flew to the duke's shoulder and leaned against his head, making crooning noises.

The duke scratched the parrot's head feathers and pictured again the amazement with which Verity would receive his proposal. That she might refuse him never entered his head.

116

Verity came in followed by the dog and the cat. She looked pale and wan.

"Pray be seated, Your Grace," she said. "Mrs. Manners is unfortunately still asleep."

"I came to see *you*," said the duke, smiling at her in a way that made poor Verity's heart lurch.

"And how may I be of service to you?" asked Verity.

He rose, lifted the parrot from his shoulder, and placed it on the back of a chair. He walked forward, took her hands in a strong clasp, and raised her to her feet.

"I shall ask your father's permission to pay my addresses to you as soon as he returns from Scotland."

Verity looked dazed. "Are you asking me to marry you?"

"Yes."

She hung her head. He gave her hands an impatient tug.

"What is your reply, Miss Bascombe?"

"No, I cannot," said Verity, pulling her hands away.

The amazement he had fondly imagined would be on Verity's face was on his own. "Why? Are you already engaged?"

"No, Your Grace."

"Then why?"

Verity longed to say yes, but loyalty to Charlotte would not let her. Made clumsy by grief and wretchedness, she said, "I don't want to marry you."

"Then I shall take my unwanted presence away. But before I go, answer me this. You allowed me to kiss you, and you enjoyed it. Are you in the habit of accepting kisses from gentlemen when your intentions are not serious?"

"Yes," said Verity. "I am a terrible flirt. Gentlemen are always kissing me."

"Good day to you, Miss Bascombe," he said in frosty accents.

"Good day," echoed Verity faintly, sitting down suddenly as if all the strength had gone out of her legs. She sat in numb despair, hearing his voice in the hall as he collected his hat and cane from Pomfret, hearing the door slam.

She tried to tell herself she had done a noble thing. Charlotte was silly and vain, but she had pledged her friendship. But life was hard and cruel.

"What a bloody life!" said Verity, trying to relieve some of her despair by swearing.

"Pretty Polly," said the parrot.

Verity stared at it. It put its head on one side and then began to speak in an excellent imitation of Charlotte's trilling voice.

"Why don't you flap along to dear Verity? I wish I had never invited Verity. I can't stand her with her oh-so-good ways. She's been making sheep's eyes at Denbigh. He *can't* be interested in her. She's such a drab little frump. I mean, compared to me, she's nothing. I never liked her, anyway—Miss Prunes and Prisms. She only pretends to be intelligent, but she's stupid really. And common! Only a country lawyer's daughter. I feel soiled by having her around. I shall continue all this 'dear Verity' friendship act until I can gracefully send her packing. I think I did well. She swallowed every word. As if one such as I could ever love one such as she! But at least I have made sure she will no longer encourage Denbigh."

The parrot fell silent. Verity rose to her feet again, approached the parrot, and took it by the throat.

"What did you say?" she demanded, shaking it.

118

"Awk," said Pretty Polly.

"Answer me!" shouted Verity.

The parrot looked at her with flat obsidian eyes.

"Tol rol," came Charlotte's amused voice from the door. "I am glad to see you are human, Verity. The times I have felt like strangling that bird myself!"

Verity swung around, fists clenched, eyes narrowed. "So it was all a trick to get me to refuse Denbigh, was it?"

"What are you talking about? Refuse Denbigh? He is not likely to propose to you."

"Well, he did, this morning, just a few moments ago, and I refused him clumsily and rudely out of loyalty to you. Pretty Polly told me everything."

"Stoopid. The bird can't say a word."

"Urk," said the parrot obligingly.

"Well, it did," howled Verity. "And you said you felt soiled by having me around. You said I was common. You said all your pleas of friendship were so that I would not encourage Denbigh. You are a monster, Charlotte."

"Stop ranting and raving like a fishwife at this ungodly hour of the day. You belong in Bedlam. The parrot can't talk, and I don't believe for a minute that Denbigh proposed. You are ugly with your face all screwed up like that. Yes, ugly. As ugly as—as ... that parrot. You can pack and get out and take those creatures with you, or I shall throw them all in the Serpentine! *Get out!*"

"I was on my way to the park when Denbigh called," said Verity. "I shall still go and make my farewells to Lady Wythe."

She pushed past Charlotte into the hall. "Pomfret!" Charlotte screamed from behind her. "Get this slut's bags packed and have them corded and waiting in the hall."

James, the second footman, held open the door and started to follow Verity. "You stay where you are," ordered Charlotte. "You are *my* servant, not hers!"

Verity moved like a sleepwalker in the direction of Hyde Park. It was sunny and warm. She felt like a blob of black misery moving through the glory of the day.

A hand came out and took the dog's leash from her. She looked up and saw James, the second footman.

"You must go back, James," she cried. "You will lose your employ."

"I think it's about time I returned to the country," said James. "Mrs. Manners's household does not suit me. If you will just walk ahead, ma'am. It don't do to be seen walking side by side with a footman."

Verity's eyes filled with tears and she blinked them away. She walked on quickly, hoping Lady Wythe would be at their usual bench.

As she walked across the park, she felt a stab of relief when she saw the erect figure of the countess sitting on the bench. She quickened her pace. She would not distress the old lady with her troubles. She would simply make her dignified good-byes.

"What ails you, child?" cried the countess, as Verity came up to her. "My dear, anything I can do to help. Please tell me."

Verity fell to her knees on the grass, all her brave resolutions to be dignified crumbling away, and buried her head in the countess's lap and cried her eyes out, while the countess patted her arm and made soothing noises.

At last, Lady Wythe said sharply, "Now, that is quite enough, Miss Bascombe. Blow your nose and then sit beside me and tell me all. At once!"

Verity did as she was bid. In a halting voice, she told her story.

Lady Wythe looked at the parrot, who was strolling up and down in front of them.

"Are you sure you did not imagine it?" she said in a wondering voice. "That creature *talk*?"

"It *did*." Verity hiccupped. "Honestly. A clear imitation of Charlotte's voice."

Lady Wythe poked the parrot in the chest with the point of her parasol. "Say something," she commanded.

"Eeerk," said the parrot huffily, and flew off.

"It *did* speak," said Verity.

"There now. Do not distress yourself. If you say it did, it did. What are your plans?"

"I shall return to Market Basset and stay with one of the neighbors, though goodness knows what they will make of these creatures."

"Stay with me," said Lady Wythe. "I mean it. I have a large mansion in Green Street." She twisted her head around and looked up at the tall footman who was standing behind the bench. "And I suppose I will need to engage you as well, young man. If Mrs. Manners has not already given you your marching orders, she will when you return."

"Thank you, ma'am," said James, looking relieved, for his family was very poor and would be distressed at the thought of having another mouth to feed.

"So," said Lady Wythe briskly. "You shall come with me, Miss Bascombe. James, you return to Berkeley Square and collect Miss Bascombe's belongings and bring them to number twenty-five Green Street."

"Very good, my lady."

"And I shall order you new livery today. I do not

want a footman of mine wearing That Woman's colors!"

When James returned to Berkeley Square, he noticed with relief that Verity's serviceable trunk was corded and standing in the hall along with the parrot's cage.

Pomfret appeared behind him. "I suppose you know I have orders to dismiss you."

"It's all right, Mr. Pomfret. Miss Bascombe has been invited to stay with the Countess of Wythe and I am to be employed by her."

The butler looked relieved. "You're a good fellow, James," he said. "Madam is in a terrible rage. I sent Paul around to the mews for the handcart, thinking you might have to go to the stage, but you can use it to push this stuff round to Green Street. Oh, lor', there's someone at the door."

The butler opened the door. Lord James Castleton presented his card and asked if Mrs. Manners was at home.

"I shall see, my lord," said Pomfret doubtfully. He gave a little jerk of his head to indicate to the footman that he had better make his escape while Mrs. Manners was still abovestairs. Then he ushered Lord James into the Yellow Saloon and went in search of his mistress.

To his surprise, Charlotte brightened at the news that Lord James had called and said she would be down directly.

When Charlotte entered the saloon, Lord James caught his breath. He did not know she was still in a towering rage. He only noticed that her blue eyes blazed like sapphires and that her cheeks were flushed a becoming pink.

"I came to present my compliments, Mrs. Manners," he said, "and also in the hope that you might care to take a drive with me."

"I should be delighted, my lord," said Charlotte dimpling up at him.

"Perhaps," he added politely, "Miss Bascombe might also—" He broke off as Charlotte's eyes flashed angry fire.

"Do not mention that creature's name," said Charlotte. "Never have I been more sadly deceived. I have sent her packing."

"What happened?"

"I don't want to talk about it," said Charlotte, proceeding to do so. "I invited her to town because I felt sorry for the poor provincial thing. Little did I know that she was eaten up with mad ambition. She lured Denbigh back to town to try to snare him for herself. And do you know how that deceitful creature did it? She knew he had once proposed to me, so she wrote him letters supposedly from me, knowing that would lure him back. Then she proceeded to flirt with him boldly and outrageously."

"No!"

"Yes," said Charlotte, dabbing her eyes. "I had thought she would have reformed. The time at school when she ran away with the fencing master . . . Let me not go on."

"Please do not. I can see you are sorely distressed."

"And then there was the music master . . . So many, many men. Woe is me. To have housed a trollop."

Charlotte burst into tears.

"Mrs. Manners, where is Miss Bascombe now?"

"She has gone home on the stage, I am glad to say." Charlotte wondered whether to accuse Verity of having stolen her pets but decided that would be going too far. She dried her eyes and summoned up a brave smile. "I think, my lord, that a little fresh air would do me a power of good."

"Of course, of course. Only too glad . . ."

"I shall fetch my bonnet," said Charlotte, once more dry-eyed.

When she had left the room, Lord James thought over what she had said. Denbigh must hear of Miss Bascombe's treachery as soon as possible.

Chapter Eight

"I trust you are not too interested in Miss Bascombe, Charles?" Lord James said later that day. He had run the duke to earth in Bright's Coffee House.

"No, I am not interested in her in the slightest."

"Good," said Lord James, pulling out a chair and sitting down next to the duke. "Poor Mrs. Manners. She was sadly deceived."

"I am beginning to think that Mrs. Manners and Miss Bascombe are two of a kind," said the duke.

"How can you compare such beauty and sweetness with conniving and plotting and lack of morals?"

"Do not be too harsh on Mrs. Manners," said the duke, raising his eyebrows. "She is hanging out for a title, that is all."

"I was not talking about Mrs. Manners," said Lord James passionately. "Do you know that Miss Bascombe wrote those letters to you without Mrs. Manners's knowledge?"

The duke looked at his friend in high irritation. "Mrs. Manners knew all about those letters. When

I praised them and thanked her for them, she did not protest but accepted all my compliments."

Lord James looked momentarily nonplussed. "Well, well," he went on, "I may have made a mistake, but Mrs. Manners did tell me that Miss Bascombe hoped to entrap you."

"Then she has a very odd way of showing it," said the duke crossly, "because I proposed marriage to Miss Bascombe and she turned me down. She accepted a kiss from me with great warmth and I was led to believe she would favor my suit, but she told me boldly that she was quite used to being kissed."

"Then that does tally with what Mrs. Manners said," cried Lord James. "For when they were at school, Miss Bascombe had an affair with the dancing master and then the fencing master."

"Indeed! Mrs. Manners was probably only being malicious. Bold as Miss Bascombe appeared to me, she still seems too levelheaded and gently bred a lady to have behaved so."

"When we were driving this afternoon, Mrs. Manners told me that Miss Bascombe likes to lead men on and then spurn them."

"If she had an affair with a schoolmaster, then that is not exactly spurning anyone."

"Did I say affair? I mean there was an involvement of some sort. I forget the exact words."

"And where is the wicked Miss Bascombe now?"

"She has been sent packing. On the stage home, I should think."

The duke registered dully that the news of Miss Bascombe's departure from London made him feel quite ill. Then he tried to rally his spirits. He did not quite believe any of Mrs. Manners's gossip, and yet he felt sure he had had a lucky escape. He would soon forget her.

"Verity!"

Charlotte burst into the bedchamber that had recently been occupied by Verity and stopped short. "Oh, I had forgot," she said. "Of course she has left."

She trailed off to her own bedchamber and sat sulkily on the edge of the bed. It was just like Verity to flounce off like that. Charlotte had attended a rout that evening. The Duke of Denbigh and Lord James had arrived late. The duke had treated her to a mere civil nod, but Lord James had been charming and attentive. Lord James was only the younger son of a duke, but was quite wealthy in his own right, having inherited a fortune and estates from an aunt. Where the duke was cold, Lord James was smiling and warm. Charlotte wanted to tell Verity this, but Verity had gone. The large house seemed empty without her.

Charlotte did not believe the duke had proposed to Verity. He had probably called to see her, Charlotte, and had said something that Verity had misinterpreted. And all that nonsense about the parrot . . .

Verity is jealous of me, thought Charlotte moodily, and that is why she tells lies. Charlotte told so many herself that she could not understand anyone who did not. She had quickly become used to talking to Verity, bragging to Verity, being accompanied by Verity. Without Verity, her own sex had steered clear of her at the rout. Not only that but various gentlemen had asked her hopefully where Verity was.

Of course, it was just like sneaky Verity to go and make herself embarrassingly popular.

But Charlotte missed her and thought it was also just like Verity to fly off in a huff over nothing at all.

"And what are your plans for this evening?" asked Lady Wythe the next day as she studied Verity's wan face.

"Plans? I have no plans. I shall probably do some sewing. There is a gown that needs altering."

"There is no point in staying on in London and moping in Green Street and ruining your eyes sewing," said the countess sharply. "The Dowager Duchess of Weams is giving a musicale tonight. I called on her earlier. Her companion, Miss Harris, is ill and so she said I could bring you to make up the numbers."

"I would really rather not go," said Verity miserably.

"Lord Byron is to be there."

Despite her misery, Verity felt her interest quickening. As the author of *Childe Harold's Pilgrimage*, Lord Byron was now famous. "*And* Lady Caroline Lamb is to be there as well," added the countess. "She is quite besotted with Byron and cares not who knows it, especially her poor husband, although she and William Lamb have been politely separated this age. Have you heard the latest scandal? No! It appears that at Devonshire House, Caroline Lamb appeared at the dinner table under the silver cover of quite the most enormous dish anyone has ever seen, the contents when the lid was lifted proving to be herself quite naked—not even an orange in her mouth, my dear. It fell flat because the gentlemen were dreadfully hungry and would rather have had roast beef than naked Caroline."

"I assume Lord Byron was not there in that case," said Verity, half shocked and half amused.

128

"He seems from his poetry to be a dark voluptuary."

"If you come this evening, you may judge for yourself." Lady Wythe wondered whether to tell Verity that not only Lord Byron would be there, but the Duke of Denbigh and Mrs. Manners as well. She decided against it. Besides, Verity might not go and the countess badly wanted to see Denbigh and Verity together to see if there was any hope of repairing the romance.

Verity wore the burgundy-colored gown. Lady Wythe insisted on lending her a garnet necklace set in old gold, a fine Norwich shawl, and a pretty painted fan with ivory sticks. Her own maid dressed Verity's soft brown hair in a becoming style of artistically disarrayed curls.

As they approached the Dowager Duchess of Weams's town house in Grosvenor Square, Verity began to feel a thrill of anticipation. She was in London, escorted by a countess, and she was going to meet Lord Byron. She thought of the sewing circle back at Market Basset and was determined to write down everything about the famous poet before she went to bed that evening.

The great house was crowded with people moving back and forth through the chain of saloons on the first floor, drinking and talking as they waited for the musicale to begin.

Verity was pleased to see many people present she knew and liked. She was chatting to a group of young people when Lady Wythe pulled her aside. "Now you shall meet Lord Byron," she said.

Verity followed her through the rooms to a shadowy corner. A knot of people parted at the old countess's approach. Sitting on a sofa was a young man who had been holding court.

"Miss Bascombe, may I present George, Lord Byron. Byron, Miss Verity Bascombe."

Verity curtsied low. "And how are you, Byron?" demanded the countess. "Woke up to find yourself famous, I hear."

Lord Byron remained silent, his eyes ranging beyond the countess as if looking for someone. Verity was disappointed in him. He looked like a nobleman playing the part of a successful poet. He was about the same age as she was herself, with a strangely pale face under a mop of chestnut curls. His mouth was scornful, and his whole attitude one of weary disdain.

"My lord," said Verity sharply, "you have not answered Lady Wythe's question."

He looked at her in haughty surprise. Then he turned his gaze on Lady Wythe. "I believe you asked me how I was. I am well."

There was the sound of a commotion behind Verity. She half turned as a thin, energetic figure burst past her, sat down on the sofa next to Lord Byron, took his hand, and looked at him, wide, hectic eyes eating him up. This, then, thought Verity, must be Lady Caroline Lamb. Her hair was very short and curled all over her head. Her eyes were enormous in her thin face. She was slight, angular, almost skinny, and exuded an air of excitable neuroticism. Lord Byron pressed her hand and sent a smoldering look down into her adoring face.

"Come, Miss Bascombe," said Lady Wythe. "I think the concert is about to begin."

They both turned about. Verity found herself looking up at the Duke of Denbigh. He gave her a cold nod. She blushed and curtsied, then moved on. Lady Wythe followed, her eyes snapping with interest.

"Verity!"

Verity stopped, looking amazed, as the vision that was Charlotte Manners floated toward her. "I thought you had left, my dear," said Charlotte. "Why did you not let me know you were still in London?"

Verity was speechless. "It could be because you threw her out," said Lady Wythe nastily.

"I ?" Charlotte's blue eyes filled with tears. "We had a few words but nothing that anyone in her right mind would take seriously. Lord James," she said, turning to that gentleman, who was at her side. "You know I would not harm my dear Verity."

Lord James looked bewildered. "No, no," he said gallantly. "You could not harm anyone except, perhaps, such a cavalier as I. A slight coldness in your beautiful eyes can pierce my very heart."

"Stoopid." Charlotte laughed, rapping him playfully with her fan.

Verity found herself wondering stupidly where Charlotte's tears had gone. One minute they had been sparkling on her cheeks, the next she was dry-eyed, dry-faced, and radiant. "I do not want to discuss it here," said Verity in a low voice.

"Of course not," trilled Charlotte, kissing her cheek. "We shall have a comfortable cose after supper."

She tripped off by Lord James's side.

"Goodness!" said Verity. "Is she quite mad?"

"She no longer has any hopes of Denbigh and has decided to settle for Lord James," said the countess. "How amusing it all is! Are you not glad you came?"

"It is not a play," said Verity tartly. "Although it may look that way to you."

"It's all Byron's fault," said Lady Wythe. "You

young things believe in too much sentimentality and romance. If you all concentrated more on a man's fortune and standing and less on romantical rubbish, you would all be happily married and less discontented. That's what we settled for in my day, and if the fellow had a good skin and a fine pair of legs, we considered ourselves doubly fortunate. When you get to your marriage bed, it's not whether he can recite poetry or not, it's what he does between the sheets."

"Lady Wythe, you are a shocking old rip."

"I am honest and practical and I know it does not do any good to go on like a Haymarket tragedy. Do try to show Denbigh you are not pining away, for heaven's sake. You are in looks tonight, Verity. A little sparkle is all you need. So sparkle!"

"I am not a chandelier," said Verity, amused despite herself.

At the other end of the room and well away from her, the Duke of Denbigh was talking to Mr. George Wilson. He knew Mr. Wilson slightly and would have exchanged a few civilities and passed on had not Mr. Wilson suddenly said, "I saw Miss Bascombe here tonight. Do you know her?"

"Yes, I do."

"Women. There is no trusting them. They lead you on and then spurn you," said Mr. Wilson passionately.

"You interest me," said the duke, looking at him curiously. "Did Miss Bascombe lead you on and then spurn you?"

"Yes," said Mr. Wilson. "She allowed me to believe she would favor my suit. She encouraged my attentions, and when I called to propose marriage, she laughed at me."

Still smarting with humiliation, Mr. Wilson had

convinced himself the parrot had not existed and that he had indeed proposed to Verity. To tell the duke about a gossiping parrot would make him feel ridiculous.

"Why should Miss Bascombe do that?" asked the duke.

"I think," said Mr. Wilson venomously, "that she is one of those females who need to foster adulation to feed their vanity."

"In that case," said the duke, "you may congratulate yourself on your escape, can you not?"

He moved away from Mr. Wilson, his mind busy. Charlotte's silly words to Lord James seeped through his mind like slow poison. He decided to teach Miss Bascombe a lesson. He would get his revenge, and perhaps, in the future, she would not give away her kisses so freely.

"Here comes Denbigh," hissed Lady Wythe. Verity's painted fan trembled in her hands. The duke took a seat next to her in the music room.

"What did you think of our famous poet, Miss Bascombe?" he asked.

"I was disappointed," said Verity, too rattled to do other than tell the truth. "I expected a real romantic, not a bogus romantic."

"I think you have it the wrong way round," he said. "*Childe Harold's Pilgrimage* was bogus romantic. George Byron is a true romantic."

"You are thinking of his affair with Lady Caroline Lamb?"

"No, I was not thinking of that much-publicized affair. How scandalous they are in public, how they flaunt their love for each other! If they were deeply in love, they would be content to confine their caresses and intimacies to the bedchamber. They are both playing their roles to the hilt: she, the woman half crazy with love over the country's most fa-
133

mous poet; he, the brooding romantic poet and wrecker of hearts and aristocratic marriages. He is lame, you know, and that contributes to his desire for adulation. Understandable in his case; less understandable in those without physical blemish. He had a very unhappy Calvinist childhood, and the women he really prefers are not creatures of romance but vulgar, hearty, and worldly ladies. There is a darkness in him, a self-destructive streak."

"He will go from strength to strength," said Verity. "It is said the Prince Regent much admires his poetry."

"Byron already has hopes of being made poet laureate, but the prince prefers the poetry of Walter Scott."

He stopped talking then, for the concert had begun. A pianist played Bach's Brandenburg Concerto no. 2 in F Major with great style and verve. Verity felt herself beginning to relax. The duke had forgiven her. There was still hope.

The pianist was followed by an Italian tenor with a liquid, melting voice. He not only sang arias from operas but Italian love songs also. Verity felt her hand taken in a firm clasp, started, and looked down nervously. Her stole was draped in folds over her lap, covering her hand. The duke had slid his hand under a fold of the shawl and was now clasping her own. Although both their hands were gloved, Verity thought she would faint from sheer exaltation. The tenor's voice soared to the heights, taking her with it.

The little rout chairs in the music room were jammed close together. Although she had not been aware of him moving, Verity felt the heat from the duke's thigh pressing against her own. She felt that she should draw away, that she should protest, but the people in the row of chairs in front of her were pressed together as intimately as lovers.

The duke was beginning to feel real hatred for Verity. His emotions were raging. He wanted to seize her in his arms and kiss her breathless; he wanted her naked body moving under his own until he had had enough of it. His hand tightened convulsively on hers and Verity let out a faint gasp. He glanced down at her. Her lips were red and slightly parted. Her bosom rose and fell quickly. He wanted to put his hands against her breasts and feel them swelling against his fingers.

The tenor finished and bowed. The audience applauded, with the exception of Verity and the duke, who sat very still, hands locked, backs straight—no one but the very vulgar ever allowed his or her back to touch the back of the chair—hip against hip, leg against leg, and both of them feeling quite sick with emotion.

People began to rise. Chattering voices rose on the air. Someone was quoting loudly from *Childe Harold*:

> "Then must I plunge again into the crowd,
>   And follow all that Peace disdains to
>   seek?
>   Where Revel calls, and Laughter, vainly
>   loud,
>   False to the heart, distorts the hollow
>   cheek . . ."

The pianist dropped the lid of the piano and picked up sheets of music; the doors of the supper room were thrown open by two liveried footmen, their faces impassive beneath their spun-glass wigs.

Lady Wythe, still talking to an elderly friend who had been seated to her left, shook out her skirts and started to walk away, then turned and looked back in surprise.

The duke and Verity were sitting, very still, both of them staring straight ahead, their eyes quite empty.

Lady Wythe gave a cluck of disapproval.

"Miss Bascombe!" she called. "Supper!"

The duke released Verity's hand and arranged her shawl about her shoulders. He smiled down into her eyes and Verity gave a timid half smile back.

In a daze of happiness, she walked beside him to the supper room.

Holding her arm under the elbow, he piloted her down the room and over to a corner of one of the long tables by the far window. There was no one sitting near them.

A waiter came up with champagne. "No, no," protested Verity. "I do not think I like champagne anymore."

"Quite right," the duke said to the waiter. "Take the stuff away and bring us a couple of bottles of port."

"I don't think I want port, either, Your Grace," protested Verity. "I do not have a good head for wine."

"It is a particular kind of port," he lied. "Not at all strong."

He chose a selection of delicacies for Verity from the trays of food presented to them and, when it arrived, filled her glass to the brim with port. Verity was surprised at the duke's taste. Although many of the old guard in society damned burgundy and claret as weak beverages only suitable for women and children, she would not have thought that the duke shared their tastes. She herself did not like the heavy sweet wine as an accompaniment to meat. But the port was giving her much-needed Dutch courage, and so she barely noticed how deftly he kept topping up her glass.

He began to talk of the American war. America, tired of the Royal Navy's blockade, had declared war on Great Britain. A British squadron, moving by river, had landed four thousand regular soldiers within reach of Washington, where they burned the capital. Strangely, this had not done much to inspire the British, said the duke, but it had infuriated the Americans, and so this odd, scattered war continued to rage apace from Canada down to Louisiana, with hastily assembled small forces advancing and retreating and losing and winning all over the place.

Verity drank a great deal and listened muzzily to his voice and studied his strong profile and was totally unaware of anyone else in the room.

When the Countess of Wythe rose to leave the supper room, she decided it was better to leave Verity with the duke. They appeared to be talking together like old friends. The dowager smiled to herself. It seemed certain that Verity Bascombe was to be the next Duchess of Denbigh.

The duke and Verity were now discussing novels. "Have you read Mrs. Baxter's *Follies of a London Lady*?" he asked.

"I have never even heard of Mrs. Baxter," said Verity, which was not surprising since the duke had just invented her.

"Oh, but you must read her. I am sure they have a copy in the library here." He stood and pulled out her chair as she rose tipsily and unsteadily to her feet. "The library is just across the hall. Let us go and have a look for it."

Verity let him lead her through the supper room, back through the music room, and across the hall. She did not think she was doing anything improper. She was dazed with port and love and happiness. He held open the door of the library, ushered her inside, and shut the door behind them.

The library was dark and quiet, the serried ranks of calf-bound books rising from floor to ceiling. In the center of the room was a long, backless sofa upholstered in red-and-gold-striped silk. On a low table in front it lay a pile of books and magazines.

"Ah, I think I see it," said the duke, pulling Verity forward. "On that table." He sat on the sofa and drew Verity down beside him.

Then he turned, looked at her with a mocking glint in his eyes, and said, "Would you be very alarmed, Miss Bascombe, if I were to tell you that there is no such creature as Mrs. Baxter and no such book?"

"Not alarmed," said Verity. "But surprised. Why should you tell such a lie?"

"To get you alone," he said, drawing her into his arms.

Verity sank against his chest with a little sigh. She could not ever remember being so happy. He had proposed once, he was about to propose again, and she loved him with all her heart. The fact that she was alone and unchaperoned in his company did not shock her. She trustingly and innocently turned her lips up to his.

He took off his gloves and tossed them onto the table. Then he bent his head and sank his mouth onto her own. One strong, white hand clasped itself around Verity's left breast. She gave a little start of alarm and began to pull away, but he was now kissing her fiercely and her body was melting and burning under his touch. He forced her back until she was lying beneath him on the sofa. His thigh slid between her legs, and his hands moved caressingly over the smoothness of her silk gown, running down the length of her body. In spite of her heady, aching passion, a cold draft of air on her legs shot a horrified message to her brain. He had raised her skirt.

His mouth was nuzzling at the neckline of her gown against her breast as one experienced hand glided slowly up her stockinged leg to the bare flesh above.

Verity gave one enormous push and toppled him off the sofa. He rolled across the low table, scattering books, before jumping nimbly to his feet. He stood with both hands on his hips, laughing down at her.

"You are quite right to stop me," he said. "I would prefer you in my bed."

Verity tugged down her skirts and stood. "I have drunk too much," she said. "You shock me, Your Grace."

"You surprise *me*, Miss Bascombe. It was interesting to find out just how far I could go before you cried halt."

"But we are to be married!" cried Verity. She was now more shocked by the mocking insolence she saw in his eyes than she had been by his over-intimate caresses.

"Don't be silly. I was stupid enough to propose to you once. But when you told me you were in the habit of being, er, generous with your kisses, I realized I could take what I wanted without having to marry you first."

"I thought you loved me!" cried Verity. "I would never have let you touch me otherwise."

"Now, now," he said soothingly, advancing on her again. "We know that is not true. You let me kiss you before."

Verity edged away. "Keep your distance," she said.

He moved quickly between her and the door.

Verity was shaken by such a wave of rage and disgust she could have killed him.

Out of the corner of her eye, she saw the white gleam of a bust on a pedestal.

She darted toward it, picked it up, and threw it at the duke, who ducked. The bust sailed over his head and crashed into smithereens on the floor.

"You hellcat," he said gratingly, advancing on her.

Verity ran to the fireplace and seized the fire irons. First she threw the poker at his head, then the tongs, then the shovel, and then the toasting fork.

He ducked and weaved, trying to get to her.

Verity picked up a vase of roses and sent it sailing at his head just as the door of the library opened and a crowd of startled guests rushed in.

Charlotte had seen them going into the library together and had told Lord James and anyone else who happened to be listening. The news quickly spread, and the guests decided it would be fun to burst in on the couple.

They arrived just in time to see the duke neatly fielding the vase of flowers.

"A romp!" cried one excitable young miss. Laughing hysterically, she pulled a volume from the shelves and threw it at the duke.

The cream of society, those sticklers for good be-

140

havior and good *ton*, leaped into the fray like children, and soon the whole library was full of screaming and laughing guests and flying books.

The duke stalked out. He wanted to get as far away from Verity Bascombe as possible, and for a reason that infuriated him. He felt he had behaved badly and disgracefully. He felt he owed her a sincere apology, and, at the same time, he was damned if she was going to get one!

"So let us go over this again," said Lady Wythe severely. "You let him take you into the library and you let him close the door. You are old enough to know that a gentleman with honorable intentions never does that. Then he kissed you, lay on top of you, and raised the hem of your gown. I must ask you again. How far up did he get?"

"Two inches above my knee. That was all. I told you and told you—"

"Humph! Are you sure he proposed *marriage* to you?"

"Yes, definitely. He said he would call on my father."

"As your father is not here, I think that Denbigh had better explain his conduct to me."

"Don't! I never want to see him again!"

"If you are going to go about with me—and I go about a great deal—you are bound to see him again. It would be better to have an explanation out of him first. Not another word. I am disappointed in you, Verity. There—I shall call you Verity. I repeat, I am disappointed. At your age, you should have learned the gentle art of repulsing bold advances. You will be tying your garter in public next!"

"I had drunk too much," said Verity. She was

141

lying in bed with the cat on one side of her and the dog on the other. Pretty Polly was perched on the bed head, looking very interested in the conversation.

"Of what? Champagne?"

"No, port."

"*Port!* Mark my words, Denbigh was hellbent on seduction, and I wonder why. He never had the reputation of being a rake. How on earth did you turn down his proposal? Did you humiliate him?"

"No, no. I was miserable, for I had sworn loyalty to Charlotte, and she had told me she was deeply in love with Denbigh. He—he said I had accepted his kiss and had led him to believe I would favor his suit, and—and . . . I replied . . ."

"Yes, yes, you replied?"

Verity hung her head. "I told him I was in the way of being kissed by gentlemen."

"Grant me patience." The countess sighed. "In other words, you as good as told him you were a trollop! But I must tax him with his behavior. We must make sure he does not talk of it. Oh, I forgot. There is this letter for you. One of Mrs. Manners's footmen delivered it. I meant to give it to you earlier today, but it went out of my mind."

Verity opened the letter and glanced at the first few sentences. "It is from Papa," she said. "Why, he has returned! I can go home."

"Not until we make sure your reputation is in the clear," said the countess severely. "Mind you, the disgrace of that romp, which half ruined a good library, will put memories of anything else out of society's silly head. I hate romps. So undignified, but usually people confine themselves to throwing cushions at each other instead of wrecking a library. I shall send for Denbigh tomorrow and you may stay abovestairs until he is gone. The trouble

is that you fancy yourself in love with him. Quite
ridiculous. A good, solid arranged marriage with
one of your own class is just what you need. I
thought Denbigh would do for you, but his behavior was disgraceful because, apart from anything
he heard or you said, he obviously considers you
beneath him.''

Verity lay awake for a long time after the countess had left. She could not believe her own wanton
behavior. He had touched her here and here. She
groaned, turned her face into the pillow, and prayed
for sleep to come.

When summoned the following morning, the
Duke of Denbigh came promptly. The countess
waited until he was seated before demanding an
explanation of his behavior.

''I usually do not listen to gossip, Lady Wythe,''
said the duke heavily, ''but when Miss Bascombe
refused my suit, she said airily that she was in the
way of being kissed by gentlemen. Then I had some
of Mrs. Manners's spite relayed to me by Lord
James. I did not want to believe it. Then last night
I met Mr. George Wilson. He told me he had proposed to Miss Bascombe and had been cruelly
turned down.''

''Nonsense. He seemed on the point of propos-
ing, but when he called, he was the one who was
rude. He told Verity that he was calling only to
say good-bye, for he was going to join his mother,
and that he hoped she did not expect a proposal
from him for he would not stoop so low, or some
such rubbish. Now, Charlotte Manners had already received some peculiar rebuffs from angry
gentlemen. Verity swears her parrot is relaying
malicious gossip to callers, but I find it hard to
believe, for the bird never says a word.''

"But what I do not understand is why, instead of taking the girl in disgust, you should set about trying to molest her—you, who could have any woman you wanted."

"My pride was damaged," he said stiffly. "I simply wanted a little mild revenge and became carried away. Pray convey my sincerest apologies to Miss Bascombe. I have always considered myself above listening to idle gossip. I do not quite know what happened to me."

"Do not let it happen again," said the countess, rising to show the interview was at an end. "Miss Bascombe is an innocent, unused to the cruel gossip or ways of society. She will shortly be returning to the country where she will be better off settling down with a worthy man of her own caste."

When the duke walked off down Green Street, his first thought was that he had escaped lightly. This was immediately followed by such a wave of physical longing for Verity Bascombe that he could have cheerfully strangled her. He wished now that he had asked Lady Wythe if she had any idea why Verity had refused his suit. He wanted to confide in someone, but men did not discuss such things. Lord James was so besotted with Charlotte he would probably tell the duke he was well out of it.

The duke made up his mind to retreat to his estates in the country. Out of sight, out of mind, he told himself severely. But a niggling, treacherous voice at the back of his brain was telling him that it would do no harm to stay in London just to see her one more time. He would find her quite an ordinary female. He would find his feelings for her had been some sort of temporary madness.

And so, like a man suffering from a strong addiction, he persuaded himself that he had only to put it to the test one more time to prove to himself that he was a free man.

Chapter Nine

Charlotte and Lord James walked slowly along the Serpentine. She had felt in her bones he was about to propose and was anxious to get him out of that house in Berkeley Square before he said a word.

It was a still, gray day. All color seemed to have been bleached out of London. The tall trees stood motionless. Even the graceful deer in their pound over to the right looked as if they had been made out of iron. The water of the Serpentine was like glass; the only thing to disturb its mirrorlike surface were the gas bubbles rising from the bottom and the disgusting floating debris on the top.

"How romántic it is!" Lord James sighed. Charlotte thought cynically of various newspaper reports complaining of the awful smell of the Serpentine because the main sewer from Bayswater debouched into it, but wisely held her tongue and raised a scented handkerchief to her nose instead.

"I am glad you are your usual beautiful self," Lord James went on. "That was a frightful scene last night."

"Yes," agreed Charlotte, wishing he would propose and get it over with. "Our London ways have gone to Verity's head. I believe it was she who started the romp by playfully throwing a vase of flowers at Denbigh."

Lord James reflected that Verity's horrified face had made her look like a woman defending her honor but considered it politic not to disagree with his beloved. He was enchanted with Charlotte's beauty. He often did not listen to what she said. It was enough just to look at her.

"I think London is not a suitable place for anyone of breeding to live," said Lord James. "So many counter-jumpers and mushrooms have invaded society."

"Where would you live?" asked Charlotte uneasily.

"I have estates in the country and a most beautiful home that only lacks a mistress to make it perfect."

"The country is only for visiting when society has left town," said Charlotte firmly.

"Of course, you are right," he cried. "Last night's episode, all the same, must surely disgust anyone with any sensibility whatsoever."

"Mmm," said Charlotte vaguely, wondering whether he meant to parade her up and down by this smelly stretch of water forever.

"Mrs. Manners," he said, stopping and turning to face her, "I do not know quite how to find the courage to . . . Alas! I dare not."

A chill little wind sprang up, ruffling the waters of the Serpentine. A rotten animal carcass rose to the surface.

"Oh, do try to say whatever it is you want to say," urged Charlotte.

"My head aches, my heart burns, I feel as if I am

147

in the grip of a fever," he cried. "Oh, that tongue might dare speak the precious words. Oh, that—"

"Yes," Charlotte said in a flat voice.

He looked down at her in surprise. "Yes what, fair one?"

"Yes, I will marry you," said Charlotte, "only the day has turned cold and I do not want to stay in Hyde Park forever."

He seized her hand and kissed it. Charlotte surveyed him while her dispassionate aristocratic eyes assessed him. Good legs and his own teeth; unmarked face. She could have fared worse.

They walked back in the direction of Berkeley Square, Lord James in a daze of happiness, Charlotte with a sense of achievement and already planning her wedding gown.

Pretty Polly flew overhead and let out a mocking squawk. Charlotte brightened. "Verity must be around somewhere."

"Do not worry," said Lord James caressingly. "We shall cut her if we see her."

Charlotte bit her lip, a lot of her pleasure in the proposal gone. It would be fun if Verity could be her bridesmaid. They could drink champagne and laugh and discuss clothes. Verity had been the only female friend Charlotte had ever had. She missed her humor, her sharp remarks; she even missed that wretched menagerie.

"We must not be too hard on poor Verity," she said. "Denbigh has behaved disgracefully."

"Charles! But, my love, you said—"

"Now, did I ever say a word against my dear Verity?"

Lord James remembered vividly every single word that Charlotte had said about Verity, but when he looked at the whiteness of her bosom, revealed by the low-cut gown she wore, the roundness of her arms, and the beauty of her eyes, he felt it did not matter one bit.

"Of course not," he said happily, and tucking her arm in his, he led her from the park.

Late that afternoon, Verity was sitting reading to Lady Wythe when the butler announced that Mrs. Manners had called to see Miss Bascombe.

"We are not at home," said the countess.

"Wait," said Verity nervously. "I would like to see her, dear Lady Wythe. Just to see what plots and plans she is making now."

Lady Wythe rose to her feet. "You want to see her because you want to be reassured that Denbigh has not proposed to her. I shall not stay here and be party to your nonsense. If you want to see her, then see her alone."

Charlotte came tripping in wearing one of the new Invisible hats, which was a circle of stretched gauze. She ran to Verity and tried to kiss her, but Verity backed away behind a chair. "State your business, Charlotte," she said.

"So hard!" cried Charlotte. "You are a most peculiar female, Verity. Hot one minute, cold the next. I have great news. I am to wed Lord James."

Verity slowly came round from behind the chair. "I thought you were after Denbigh."

"And so I was. But it is hopeless. He is a strange man, and after the way he treated you last night—shocking!—I quite put him from my mind."

"My felicitations, Charlotte. But why have you come? Can you possibly have forgotten the way you treated me?"

"I do not know what you are talking about," said Charlotte, opening her blue eyes to their widest. "Did I not invite you to London? Did I not take you everywhere? You rewarded me by shouting insults at me and walking out. But I am prepared to forgive you."

"Charlotte, you are quite mad."

Charlotte gave a ripple of laughter. "There! You have the right of it. So we can be friends and you can be my bridesmaid."

"Thank you, but I must refuse."

"Why?"

Verity gritted her teeth. "Because," she said firmly, "I do not like you, Charlotte."

"Oh, oh, oh!" shrieked Charlotte, and then burst into floods of tears.

Verity looked at her helplessly. "Do pull yourself together, Charlotte."

Charlotte continued to sob. She slumped down in a chair, looking the very picture of beauty in distress. Her crying became louder and harsher, and sobs shook her body.

Verity became alarmed and rang the bell. James, now a first footman, came in. "James, fetch the hartshorn," said Verity. "Mrs. Manners is having a spasm."

"No, no." Charlotte coughed. "Brandy, I beg of you."

James went hurrying off. Verity knelt on the floor beside Charlotte and gently took her hands. "Please do not cry, Charlotte. You must not be so sorely distressed."

Charlotte leaned her head heavily on Verity's shoulder and continued to cry. The action crumpled her new hat and that worried Verity more than anything else. Charlotte must indeed be very upset to ruin a good hat. She patted her on the back and looked up with relief when James came in with a decanter of brandy and two glasses.

Verity sent him away and detached herself from Charlotte. She poured a stiff measure into one of the glasses and held it to Charlotte's lips. How someone could sob and cry and yet drain a stiff measure of spirits was amazing to Verity. She thought it must be an acquired social grace, like learning to always sit down on a chair without looking behind you or to eat asparagus without letting the butter run down your chin. "More," whispered Charlotte weakly. "My nerves."

Verity gave her another glass, then poured one for herself with a shaking hand and drained it off.

"I miss you, Verity," mumbled Charlotte.

Verity's kind heart was touched. Charlotte was very spoiled and willful, but she was not going to marry Denbigh. That glorious thought finally sank into Verity's mind. She felt she could forgive Charlotte anything.

"We will let bygones be bygones," said Verity. "Do not cry, Charlotte. If my father gives me permission, I will be the bridesmaid at your wedding."

It was like watching a butterfly emerging from a chrysalis, marveled Verity, as the crumpled, sobbing heap in the chair slowly straightened up, stopped crying abruptly, straightened her hat, poured another glass of brandy, winked at Verity over the rim, and knocked it back with a practiced twist of the wrist.

"We shall have such fun!" cried Charlotte. "Now, you know the veil is quite outmoded. No one who is anyone gets married in church these days. But I think it might prove vastly fashionable to do unfashionable things. I shall have a veil of Brussels lace and be married in St. George's, Hanover Square. Oh, and a *very* long train. Do you think you could manage a long train?"

She prattled on. Verity drank another glass of brandy to sustain herself and wondered what on earth Lady Wythe was going to say when she learned that Verity had agreed to be Charlotte's bridemaid.

"And you *reek* of brandy," Lady Wythe ended crossly after raging at Verity for half an hour. She had been unable to believe her ears when Verity had told her of the renewed friendship. "I tell you this, Verity Bascombe, society was amused because the stupid Mrs. Manners had such a clever and bright companion, but *she* is the clever one and you have as much brains as that parrot of yours. Thank goodness nothing came of that business with Denbigh. You! A duchess. Saints preserve us, you wouldn't have the faintest idea how to go on. You are going to be taught a lesson. I am going to give a dinner party for the highest sticklers in London society, including Denbigh. Mark how we go on, mark the difference between us and you, Verity Bascombe, and wonder that you ever thought to marry a duke!"

"What a nasty thing to say, you old termagant," said Verity, rallying. "You encouraged me to fall in love with Denbigh. People are just people, no matter what their rank. There are good and bad, common and vulgar people, saints and sinners in every walk of life."

"Heavens! I have housed a radical."

"No, you have housed someone who will not put up with your insults. You have said because of my birth that I am not your equal. You ought to be ashamed of yourself."

"There! Do not fly out at me. I like a girl with spirit, and I admire yours. It is my love and concern for you that make me oversharp in my speech."

Verity looked amused. "Now, I am going to insult *you*, Lady Wythe. Has it ever dawned on you

152

that you and Mrs. Manners have a great deal in common . . . ?"

Two weeks passed, and although Verity went everywhere with Lady Wythe, she did not see the Duke of Denbigh. At last, she began to feel an easing of the pain in her heart. Good sense took over. A man who treated her so wantonly was a man to be avoided at all costs. Her treacherous body, which previously had shown alarming signs of wishing the duke would inflict those disgusting intimacies on it again, settled down, like a burned-out fire settling in the hearth.

And then a letter arrived from her father. He was in high alt to learn she was the houseguest of a countess and begged her to remain in London for as long as she liked. But the rest of his letter made Verity exclaim in dismay. Emily Butterworth had written to her father while he was in Scotland, tender and charming letters, Mr. Bascombe said. He had proposed to Emily on his return and she had accepted him. Verity put down the letter. She was to have a stepmother the same age as herself. Emily was pleasant and friendly, but Verity knew her old life had gone. Emily would be the mistress of the household and she the unwanted spinster intruding on her father's happiness. She had a sharp longing for her mother. She did not blame her father for not remaining faithful to the memory of his dead wife, yet she had never imagined he really would marry again.

Verity was fond of Lady Wythe, but nevertheless she did not quite trust her friendship. She, Verity, was a novelty that kept the old countess amused. Verity often felt that the countess might one day soon become as bored with her as she had initially been delighted with her company.

* * *

The Duke of Denbigh had allowed his common sense to prevail and had taken himself back to his stately home in the country. The memory of Verity was dimmed by distance. Shame at his own behavior made him want to forget her, and he prided himself on having done the sensible thing. And then he received a card from the Countess of Wythe inviting him to dinner. It was simply a gold-embossed card. There was no letter to explain why the old countess obviously expected him to uproot himself from the country and ride to London to attend a dinner party in three days' time.

He pulled forward a sheet of paper to send a courteous refusal. And then he felt Verity's lips against his own. The sensation was so vivid that he half closed his eyes. Damn her!

He pushed the sheet of paper away. He would not go. He would not even trouble to reply. He had tried to get her drunk. He had only meant to teach her a lesson, but his feelings had overcome him. He would have gladly seduced her if he had been allowed the chance.

For the next day, he worked hard on his estates, hoping physical work would ease the torment in his brain. He could not help hoping that she might be disappointed when he did not arrive.

"No word from Denbigh," said the countess, entering the drawing room where Verity was reading.

Verity looked up, startled. "Were you expecting word?"

"Yes, I invited him to my dinner party. You remember, I told you about it."

"I remember your idea was to invite him plus the cream of society in order to illustrate to me what a lowly creature I am."

154

"Well, that was wrong of me and I apologize, but I am holding a dinner party just the same and I found out he had retreated to the country, but I thought he might have troubled to send some sort of reply."

The smoldering ashes of Verity's dying passions suddenly felt as if someone had poured a can of whale oil on them. Once, at home, when the fire would not draw, her father had drained off one of the oil lamps into a jug and had thrown the contents into the fireplace. There had been a great *whumph* and then a tremendous sheet of flame. Her hands shook so hard that she hid them under her book.

Surprised that her own voice sounded so even and calm, Verity said, "Have you time to invite some other gentleman to make up the numbers?"

"No, but it does not matter. I have two extra gentlemen as it is. I always did like an excess of gentlemen at dinner," added the countess, as if discussing cookery instead of guests. "Have you a new gown to grace the affair, or have you been spending all your time racketing about the shops with the poisonous Mrs. Manners?"

"Charlotte has been amusing company of late," said Verity. "But I have made myself a gown that will be eminently suitable, although I did not anticipate your dinner party."

"What color?"

"Green. A sort of leaf-green. Vastly pretty. The finest India muslin."

"Then you shall borrow my emeralds. No, No. I insist. It is good for jewels to have an airing. And talking of airings, you should not run in the park with the dog and the cat. Most unbecoming. Mrs. French said she saw you the other day running about and throwing sticks for the dog. She said she could see your ankles."

"Then she must have been lying on the ground," said Verity tartly. "My skirts are long enough."

"You are too old to frolic, and you will soon be wearing caps."

"Yes," said Verity dismally. She had a sudden vision of herself as an elderly eccentric in a high muslin cap with a parrot on her shoulder.

The Duke of Denbigh raced toward London at breakneck speed. It seemed as if one minute he had been helping at one of his tenant's farms with the drainage, standing dressed only in leather breeches, top boots, and his shirt open at the neck; and the next he had found himself running like a madman toward his home, shouting for his racing curricle to be brought around.

In order to reach the Countess of Wythe's in time for her dinner party, he would need to ride through the rest of the day and all of the night, only stopping briefly at a posting house outside London on the day after that in order to change into his evening clothes. His town house was closed up and all of his servants had removed to the country. Of course, he could have gone to his town house and unlocked it himself. He had his valet with him. But he could not bear to think of the time it would take to heat cans of water, and a posting house would have such luxuries ready and waiting.

He made such good time that he presented himself in Green Street a full half hour before anyone was expected. The intelligence of his arrival was conveyed upstairs to the startled countess.

"Do not tell Miss Bascombe," she said to her butler, fearing that Verity might run down to see him.

"Serve him wine and biscuits and tell him I shall be with him directly."

Feeling rather silly, the duke sat in the countess's drawing room and sipped a glass of canary. Why had he come? Now that he was here, he doubted whether he even wanted to see Verity, let alone hear her voice again. Who was she, anyway? Some little provincial, not precisely pretty, hardly a Circe. But then he found himself thinking of the soft sensuality of her body. It was a wicked body, he thought crossly, and ought to be chained and padlocked. There was nothing precisely remarkable about her figure, but there was something in the way she moved that whispered promises of unbridled passion such as men dreamed of and hardly ever found.

A rattling sound disturbed his thoughts. He looked up. The parrot was sitting in a large gilt cage on a stand at the other side of the fireplace. As he watched, it put one claw through the bars and deftly unclicked the lock of its cage. It fluttered down onto the floor beside him, put its head to one side, and looked up at him.

The duke was amused. He thought the parrot looked like an elderly barrister surveying the jury with his hands clasped behind his back.

"Good evening, Polly," said the duke politely. "Say something."

"Urk," said the parrot.

"Say Pretty Polly."

The parrot turned its back on him.

"You are like your mistress," said the duke bitterly. "There's no understanding you. Bloody women!"

The parrot turned around and looked at him. "Pretty Polly," it squawked. And then it began to talk in Verity's voice. The parrot had listened in to

157

many of Verity's sad monologues, for she often consoled herself by talking her thoughts out loud to the parrot. It proceeded to treat the duke to one of the best examples.

"Oh, Pretty Polly, I think my heart is breaking," said the parrot-Verity. "I love Denbigh so much and I only turned him down out of loyalty to Charlotte. Charlotte tricked me in her usual dizzy way by claiming to be in love with Denbigh herself, and I believed her. If only he would look at me again. But he won't, Polly, for I told him a stupid thing about a lot of men having kissed me, but he was the only one, the only one ever, Polly."

The duke put his glass down with a sharp click on the marble table next to him, his heart hammering. Had he imagined it? He must have imagined it. But the parrot had spoken. "Say something else," he urged, "so that I know I am not dreaming."

The parrot gave him a bored look and began to preen its tail feathers.

"What started you off?" wondered the duke aloud. "Was it something I said? Mistress? Women?"

"Erk," the parrot said obligingly. It fluttered onto his shoulder.

"Get your bloody claws off my best evening coat," snapped the duke.

"Pretty Polly," said the parrot. The hand that the duke had raised to shove the parrot away remained in midair.

In an imitation of the countess's voice, the parrot said scornfully, "I am going to give a dinner party for the highest sticklers in London society, including Denbigh. Mark how we go on, mark the difference between us and you, Verity Bascombe, and wonder that you ever thought to marry a duke!"

The stairs outside creaked as the countess made her way down slowly. The parrot flew into its cage and slammed the door behind it.

The duke looked at it in awe. He felt a primitive desire to cross himself.

Lady Wythe came into the room and he stood to meet her, giving her his apology for arriving early.

"No matter," said the countess. "My own apologies for leaving you so long to amuse yourself."

"I was not alone. I had the parrot."

"All that thing ever does is eat and excrete. Nasty thing."

"It is a quite amazing mimic," said the duke.

"Do not tease me. That creature cannot say a word. I am glad you have come, Denbigh. It will show little Verity that you are prepared to forget that painful incident. I have arranged a beau for her, but I did not tell her—you know how stubborn and wayward girls can be these days. Eminently suitable. Mr. Sutcliffe, a rising young barrister. Very clever and bright. Just the thing for Verity."

She looked up crossly at the duke wondering whether he was foxed. The duke was turning over the parrot-Verity's words in his mind. A glow was spreading through his whole body.

The door opened and Verity came in. She was wearing a leaf-green muslin gown over a white silk underdress. Her slim neck was encircled with a choker of emeralds set in gold; emerald bracelets encircled her gloved wrists. She wore a coronet of dull gold silk flowers with green silk leaves.

She stopped short at the sight of the duke, then rallied and dropped him a curtsy.

He bent over her gloved hand and kissed it, then raised his head and smiled down into her eyes, still holding tightly on to her hand. She looked up at him warily. How beautiful her black eyes are, he thought. "I had always thought black eyes expressionless, Miss Bascombe," he said softly, "but yours are like a summer night. Tell me I am forgiven and smile on me. I would not harm you for the world."

"What are you saying?" snapped the countess.

"You are forgiven," said Verity. "I must apologize. I said that nonsense about gentlemen kissing me. I said the first stupid thing that came into my head. I gave you the wrong impression."

"Then we are friends?"

"Yes, Your Grace."

Other guests were crowding into the room. "Miss Bascombe," commanded the countess, glaring at the duke, who was still holding Verity's hand. "Here is someone I want you to meet."

The duke released her hand. Verity turned to face a handsome young man. He was correctly, if soberly, dressed, quite short in stature but with a slim figure, and a strong, square face and black hair cut in a Brutus crop. The countess introduced him as Mr. Sutcliffe and then drew the duke away to talk to her other guests.

Verity listened to Mr. Sutcliffe in an abstracted way. A footman handed Verity a glass of lemonade—the countess's instructions. Ever since Verity had drunk brandy with Charlotte, the countess had suspected her of being too heavy a drinker. But Verity felt as if she had drunk a bottle of champagne. A dizzying happiness was taking hold of her.

Mr. Sutcliffe liked to talk. He thought Verity's silence meant she was listening to his every word and began to enjoy himself.

When they went in to dinner, he was disappointed to find that he was not to sit next to the charming Miss Bascombe. The countess had placed Verity next to the duke, thinking that proximity would do the couple good and persuade Verity that a man like Mr. Sutcliffe was much more suitable. She was pleased to note that the duke talked mostly to the old lady on the other side of him and Verity to the gentleman on her left. Nothing to worry about there. The countess firmly believed that any interest the duke could have in Verity could only be of the dishonorable kind and was relieved to see he was betraying not a sign of that nonsense. She often blamed herself for having raised false hopes in Verity's bosom.

But there were all sorts of things going on that the countess could not see.

Verity's elbow brushed against the duke's and she shivered with emotion at this lightest of touches. Her napkin slipped from her lap. She moved her hand quickly to retrieve it, the duke moved his hand at the same time and his hand fell on her thigh. He apologized quickly and turned his attention back to the elderly lady on his other side, who was wont to claim long after that the Duke of Denbigh suffered from asthma, for his breathing at times was quite ragged.

Verity had planned to drink very little wine, but Mr. Sutcliffe decided to ask her to take wine with him. This taking of wine happened when one of the other guests raised his or her glass and said to someone, "Will you take wine with me?" Verity was put in the position of having to drink a great deal, for Mr. Sutcliffe kept raising his glass and toasting her and manners decreed that Verity had to toast him back and drain her glass. She hoped the wine would dull her emotions, but instead it seemed to make them more intense.

The countess had twenty-four guests seated around a table that could only hold sixteen in comfort. They were all pressed together, elbows colliding with elbows as they ate. The duke found his leg pressed against that of the old lady, who looked up at him with a surprising look in her eye that could only be described as come-hither. The duke apologized and swung his knees in the other direction and collided with Verity. Verity started and moved away from him, only to find herself pressed too close to the man on her other side, who smiled at her and moistened his lips in a way she did not like. She shifted away from him and was back to being pressed against the duke. She stayed where she was and gave herself up to the quite dreadful emotions that were tearing through her body.

At last, the countess rose to lead the ladies to the drawing room. Mr. Sutcliffe poured himself a glass of port and laid forth. He was excited to find himself in such exalted company. He had a great fund of rather warm stories and he planned to air them all.

To his great irritation, the Duke of Denbigh interrupted one of Mr. Sutcliffe's best offerings and said they should join the ladies.

The countess moodily watched the duke crossing directly to Verity's side. She wished she had invited some younger women. There was no one to take the duke's attention away from Verity. The countess even began to wish she had invited Charlotte. She walked over and placed herself firmly next to the duke, then ordered Verity to the pianoforte and made her play to entertain the guests for the rest of the evening.

But the countess decided the evening was not a total disaster. Mr. Sutcliffe asked her permission to take Verity driving in two days' time, and the countess gleefully agreed.

The duke was wearing a large signet ring. When no one was looking, he took it from his finger and slid it behind the back of the sofa cushions.

At last the guests made their farewells. Verity looked at the duke's retreating back with her heart in her eyes. He had said nothing about seeing her again.

She sat up over the tea tray, bravely pretending to be pleased over the proposed drive with Mr. Sutcliffe but relieved beyond measure when she was allowed to retire.

She tossed and turned, trying to sleep, turning the duke's words and how he had looked over and over in her head.

Then there came a scratching at the door. "Come in," she called, sitting up in bed. James, the footman, came in. "The Duke of Denbigh is belowstairs, miss," he said in a whisper. "His Grace is in ever such a taking. He says he must have lost his signet ring here and suggested you might remember where he was sitting. He doesn't want her ladyship roused."

"Tell him I will be with him soon," said Verity. When James had left, she pulled on a frilly wrapper over her nightgown, took off the plain nightcap she was wearing and changed it for a frivolous lace concoction, and then made her way down to the drawing room.

The duke was seated on the sofa. "That will be all, James," he said firmly. James, fingering a sovereign in his pocket, bowed and went out and closed the door on them.

Verity went to open the door, but the duke's voice stopped her. "Come here, my love," he said.

"Your ring?"

He held it up. "I knew where it was all the time. And we are chaperoned." He pointed to the parrot, which had flown into the room as Verity entered it. He had debated whether to tell Verity about the parrot's speech but had decided against it. He felt

163

Verity would be terribly embarrassed if she learned what the bird had said.

"You are not going to attack me again?" said Verity nervously.

"No, my heart, but I cannot sleep until I know your answer. Will you marry me?"

"Oh, *yes*," said Verity, flying toward him.

His arms closed tightly about her. "I do not think one kiss would do any harm," he said huskily.

His lips were cool and firm against her own. There was nothing to alarm her there, only a quiet tenderness. She gave a happy sigh and wound her arms about his neck and kissed him back. It was like a match thrown into a dry forest. Flame met flame. Passion met passion; hot body fused with hot body as they swayed like wrestlers, insatiable and desperate.

They slowly sank together onto the floor, wound tightly about each other, freeing their mouths only to gasp endearments, pressing hard against each other, and driving each other to distraction.

"This will not do," he said shakily. "A special license, Verity. I shall send for your father. Marry me very soon."

"Yes, Charles."

"Come driving with me tomorrow. We shall face the countess together after that and tell her our news."

"Yes, Charles."

"What a good wife you will make. Are you going to say yes to everything?"

"Yes, no . . . I don't know . . . kiss me again."

The countess was startled when the duke called the next day. But she could hardly cry out against him taking Verity out for a drive in the park in an open carriage. He could not possibly get up to anything in the middle of Hyde Park.

As they drove off, Verity let out a little cry of dismay. "I promised Charlotte I would go shopping with her this afternoon. I am to be her bridesmaid."

"Then I shall drive you to Berkeley Square and you may tell her you are otherwise engaged," said the duke. "I do not approve of your friendship with Mrs. Manners, my love."

"Oh, she is really very fond of me under all her nonsense," said Verity.

"I am glad you are not a man, Verity," said the duke as he swung his carriage in the direction of Berkeley Square, "but if you were, I think I would find you very like a professor I knew at Oxford."

"In what way?"

"Well, he was very well read and academically very clever. A highly intelligent man. But when it came to people, he was quite lacking in common sense. He lived with a spinster sister. She made sure he stayed unwed and yet he refused to believe a word against her, for she would cry most pathetically and say how devoted she was to him."

"It is not like that at all!" exclaimed Verity. "I know Charlotte can be devious and lie. I am not a fool. But there is a very real affection there."

When they reached Berkeley Square, the duke helped her down from the carriage. "Do not forget to tell her the glad news," he said blandly. "I am sure she will be delighted to be the first to know. I shall wait here in the carriage for you."

Verity ran happily up the steps and knocked at the door. Charlotte was pacing up and down the Yellow Saloon, her hat in her hand. "Oh, there you are!" she cried when she saw Verity. "Where have you been?"

"My dear friend," said Verity. "I cannot come

165

with you, but for a wonderful reason. I am engaged to Denbigh."

"You're what?" Charlotte's eyes had narrowed into slits.

"I am engaged to be married to Denbigh."

Charlotte took a deep breath. "You sly and devious creature," she raged. "You have been plotting and scheming behind my back. I see it all now. He would have been mine had it not been for you. Now you are to be a duchess and you will take precedence over me. It is past bearing. Get out of here and never let me see your treacherous face again."

The duke looked sympathetically at his beloved's white face as he helped her back into the carriage.

"I heard a crash," he said. "What was it?"

"A very pretty ornament," said Verity sadly. "Fortunately, she missed me."

"I am glad you are not going to be her bridesmaid," he said cheerfully.

"Am I so very stupid?" Verity said in a low voice. "Not about me."

He drove into the park and then across the grass and under the trees, well out of sight of the fashionable people.

He reined in and looked around. There was no one in sight. He tilted up her chin. "This is all you need," he said, and began to kiss her while one of his horses looked over its shoulder at them in surprise.

The Countess of Wythe faced the happy couple an hour later. She noticed that Verity's lips were swollen and bruised and that her eyes had a dazed look.

"Of course you have my permission, Denbigh," said the dowager crossly. "I must admit I am very surprised. Poor Mr. Sutcliffe. So suitable. Such a waste. But promise me you have behaved as a gentleman should behave with a virgin, Denbigh."

The duke gave her a limpid look. "Of course."

After he had left and Verity had floated up the stairs on a cloud of love, the countess paced up and down the drawing room. She noticed the parrot fiddling with the door of its cage and went to let it out. "Go to your mistress," she said, standing with her hand on the latch. "Oh, dear, I hope Denbigh did not do anything he should not. I shall have to act as her parent until her father arrives. But he gave me his word. Men. Bloody men!"

"Pretty Polly," said the parrot, and then in the duke's voice, "Oh, Verity, my angel, your breasts are like—"

But that was as far as the parrot got. The appalled countess swung her shawl from her shoulders and covered the cage.

There's an epidemic with 27 million victims. And no visible symptoms.

It's an epidemic of people who can't read.

Believe it or not, 27 million Americans are functionally illiterate, about one adult in five.

The solution to this problem is you... when you join the fight against illiteracy. So call the Coalition for Literacy at toll-free **1-800-228-8813** and volunteer.

Volunteer Against Illiteracy. The only degree you need is a degree of caring.

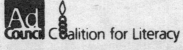

Ad Council · Coalition for Literacy

LV-1